Current Controversies

Space

Tourism, Competition, Militarization

Other Books in the Current Controversies Series

America's Role in a Changing World
Artificial Intelligence and the Future of Humanity
Big Tech and Democracy
The Business of College Sports: Who Earns What
The Capitol Riot: Fragile Democracy
Climate Change and Biodiversity
Cyberterrorism
Domestic Extremism
Media Trustworthiness
The Politics and Science of COVID-19
Reparations for Black Americans

Current
CONTROVERSIES

Space

Tourism, Competition, Militarization

Erica Grove, Book Editor

GREENHAVEN
PUBLISHING

Published in 2023 by Greenhaven Publishing, LLC
29 E. 21st Street
New York, NY 10010

First Edition

Cover image: DanieleGay/Shutterstock.com

Library of Congress Cataloging-in-Publication Data

Names: Grove, Erica M., editor.
Title: Space : tourism, competition, militarization / Erica Grove, book editor.
Description: First edition. | New York : Greenhaven Publishing, 2023. | Series: Current controversies | Includes bibliographical references and index. | Audience: Ages 15+ | Audience: Grades 10–12 | Summary: "Anthology of essays exploring the potential of space travel today"— Provided by publisher.
Identifiers: LCCN 2021055906 (print) | LCCN 2021055907 (ebook) | ISBN 9781534508835 (library binding) | ISBN 9781534508828 (paperback) | ISBN 9781534508842 (ebook)
Subjects: LCSH: Space tourism—Juvenile literature.
Classification: LCC TL793 .S693 2023 (print) | LCC TL793 (ebook) | DDC 910.919—dc23/eng/20220110
LC record available at https://lccn.loc.gov/2021055906
LC ebook record available at https://lccn.loc.gov/2021055907

Manufactured in the United States of America

Website: http://greenhavenpublishing.com

Contents

Foreword

"Controversy" is a word that has an undeniably unpleasant connotation. It carries a definite negative charge. Controversy can spoil family gatherings, spread a chill around classroom and campus discussion, inflame public discourse, open raw civic wounds, and lead to the ouster of public officials. We often feel that controversy is almost akin to bad manners, a rude and shocking eruption of that which must not be spoken or thought of in polite, tightly guarded society. To avoid controversy, to quell controversy, is often seen as a public good, a victory for etiquette, perhaps even a moral or ethical imperative.

Yet the studious, deliberate avoidance of controversy is also a whitewashing, a denial, a death threat to democracy. It is a false sterilizing and sanitizing and superficial ordering of the messy, ragged, chaotic, at times ugly processes by which a healthy democracy identifies and confronts challenges, engages in passionate debate about appropriate approaches and solutions, and arrives at something like a consensus and a broadly accepted and supported way forward. Controversy is the megaphone, the speaker's corner, the public square through which the citizenry finds and uses its voice. Controversy is the life's blood of our democracy and absolutely essential to the vibrant health of our society.

Our present age is certainly no stranger to controversy. We are consumed by fierce debates about technology, privacy, political correctness, poverty, violence, crime and policing, guns, immigration, civil and human rights, terrorism, militarism, environmental protection, and gender and racial equality. Loudly competing voices are raised every day, shouting opposing opinions, putting forth competing agendas, and summoning starkly different visions of a utopian or dystopian future. Often these voices attempt to shout the others down; there is precious little listening and considering among the cacophonous din. Yet listening and considering, too, are essential to the health of a democracy. If controversy is democracy's lusty lifeblood, respectful listening and careful thought are its higher faculties, its brain, its conscience.

Current Controversies does not shy away from or attempt to hush the loudly competing voices. It seeks to provide readers with as wide and representative as possible a range of articulate voices on any given controversy of the day, separates each one out to allow it to be heard clearly and fairly, and encourages careful listening to each of these well-crafted, thoughtfully expressed opinions, supplied by some of today's leading academics, thinkers, analysts, politicians, policy makers, economists, activists, change agents, and advocates. Only after listening to a wide range of opinions on an issue, evaluating the strengths and weaknesses of each argument, assessing how well the facts and available evidence mesh with the stated opinions and conclusions, and thoughtfully and critically examining one's own beliefs and conscience can the reader begin to arrive at his or her own conclusions and articulate his or her own stance on the spotlighted controversy.

This process is facilitated and supported in each Current Controversies volume by an introduction and chapter overviews that provide readers with the essential context they need to begin engaging with the spotlighted controversies, with the debates surrounding them, and with their own perhaps shifting or nascent opinions on them. Chapters are organized around several key questions that are answered with diverse opinions representing all points on the political spectrum. In its content, organization, and methodology, readers are encouraged to determine the authors' point of view and purpose, interrogate and analyze the various arguments and their rhetoric and structure, evaluate the arguments' strengths and weaknesses, test their claims against available facts and evidence, judge the validity of the reasoning, and bring into clearer, sharper focus the reader's own beliefs and conclusions and how they may differ from or align with those in the collection or those of classmates.

Research has shown that reading comprehension skills improve dramatically when students are provided with compelling, intriguing, and relevant "discussable" texts. The subject matter of these collections could not be more compelling, intriguing, or urgently relevant to today's students and the world they are poised to inherit. The anthologized articles also provide the basis for stimulating, lively, and passionate classroom debates. Students who are compelled to anticipate objections to their own argument and identify the flaws in those of an opponent read more carefully, think more critically, and steep themselves in relevant context, facts, and information more thoroughly. In short, using discussable text of the kind provided by every single volume in the Current Controversies series encourages close reading, facilitates reading comprehension, fosters research, strengthens critical thinking, and greatly enlivens and energizes classroom discussion and participation. The entire learning process is deepened, extended, and strengthened.

If we are to foster a knowledgeable, responsible, active, and engaged citizenry, we must provide readers with the intellectual, interpretive, and critical-thinking tools and experience necessary to make sense of the world around them and of the all-important debates and arguments that inform it. We must encourage them not to run away from or attempt to quell controversy but to embrace it in a responsible, conscientious, and thoughtful way, to sharpen and strengthen their own informed opinions by listening to and critically analyzing those of others. This series encourages respectful engagement with and analysis of current controversies and competing opinions and fosters a resulting increase in the strength and rigor of one's own opinions and stances. As such, it helps readers assume their rightful place in the public square and provides them with the skills necessary to uphold their awesome responsibility—guaranteeing the continued and future health of a vital, vibrant, and free democracy.

Introduction

> *"Space is for everybody. It's not just for a few people in science or math, or for a select group of astronauts. That's our new frontier out there, and it's everybody's business to know about space."*
>
> *—Christa McAuliffe, American astronaut and teacher*

On October 4, 1957, humankind made its first successful space launch. It was the height of the Cold War—a time of great political tension between the United States and the Soviet Union (USSR) that lasted from 1947 to 1991—and the Soviet Union had launched the *Sputnik* satellite into orbit. The USSR further solidified its superiority in this realm by launching the first man into space in 1961. However, the US met the challenge set forth by the USSR in 1969, when it landed the first man on the moon.[1] Predictably, tension between the two geopolitical powerhouses only continued to mount after these massive technological achievements, and with it grew a sense of competition in the development of space technology.

The Cold War was largely fueled by the fear of nuclear war and the desire to develop increasingly advanced weapons to defend against the adversary's nuclear warheads. Space technology and nuclear war were intertwined because the same technology that could launch a satellite or rocket into space could ostensibly be used to send a nuclear bomb to the other side of the world, which led to the Cold War's "space race." The "space race" was a series of technological innovations from the US and USSR that resulted from the rivalry and competition between the two countries to develop superior spaceflight technology, and for this reason there has been a strong link between space technology and militarization since the advent of spaceflight.[2]

Even though the Cold War has been over for decades, the relationship between space travel and militarization has persisted and shaped the space industry. In fact, this relationship even predates the Cold War, since NASA's precursor—the National Advisory Committee for Aeronautics (NACA)—was established in 1915 by a mix of military personnel and industry leaders and helped develop a wide range of military aircraft technology.[3] Eventually, NACA became the civilian agency known as the National Aeronautics and Space Administration (NASA) in 1958.

NASA continued to maintain strong ties with the military.[4] Though peaceful scientific missions make up a significant portion of the agency's operations, NASA has collaborated with the military on numerous projects, and most NASA astronauts have ties to the military as former service members.[5]

The military's reach into space extends beyond its relationship to NASA, however. In 1982, the Air Force Space Command was created by the US Air Force to assist with missile surveillance, military satellite launches and operations, and space surveillance.[6] It served this function until 2019, when the US Space Force was established as the sixth branch of the US armed forces. Although the US Space Force continues to work in conjunction with the Air Force, it is now the branch that is responsible for operating and defending military satellites and monitoring space debris.[7] As these core functions suggest, the military's activities in space are not oriented around sending weapons into space but rather defending US satellites from attacks and rubble floating through space. This is largely the case for military operations around the world due to the Outer Space Treaty, which was agreed upon in the United Nations in 1967 and was signed by 111 countries and ratified by 105 of them by 2020.[8] The Outer Space Treaty is a binding agreement between countries that establishes which space-related activities are permitted.

Among the core principles of the Outer Space Treaty is that weapons of mass destruction cannot be launched into space and set into orbit or placed on a planetary body.[9] Though at this time no countries have violated the treaty by sending nuclear weapons to space, the weaponization of space has still occurred in other ways. Many militaries use satellite technology to operate weapons on Earth, and activities from some countries have fallen into questionable territory, as demonstrated by a potential treaty violation in 2007 when China shot down one of its own satellites with a ballistic missile.[10] Some argue that the Outer Space Treaty defines prohibited activities too vaguely, while others argue that it is difficult to enforce because there is no international "space police" to keep countries in check.[11] Others assert that the treaty is outdated because it overlooks the fact that many of the major players in contemporary space exploration are not countries—they are private companies.

The exploration and use of space for commercial purposes seems poised to exponentially increase in the coming years. Historically, most commercial space activity has been in the "space-for-earth" economy, which includes internet and telecommunication infrastructure. This accounted for 95 percent of the space sector revenue in 2019.[12] While this part of the commercial space industry will likely continue to grow, another aspect of it is also on the ascent: private space travel, and space tourism in particular. The first space tourist was US millionaire Dennis Tito, who flew on a Russian rocket to the International Space Station on April 30, 2001.[13] This trip cost Tito $20 million. Since then, three space tourism companies have emerged as leaders in the industry and have successfully launched space tourist flights: Virgin Galactic (which is owned by the British billionaire Richard Branson), Blue Origin (owned by the American billionaire Jeff Bezos), and SpaceX (owned by South African–born American billionaire Elon Musk).[14]

The economic potential for commercial space travel is significant, as the Swiss investment bank UBS predicts that high-speed outer space travel will soon become a $20 billion market and that space tourism will generate at least $3 billion annually by 2030.[15] However, despite the substantial growth in this industry, the lack of regulation from the government is considered cause for alarm by some. In 2004, the US Congress passed a moratorium—or temporary prohibition—on safety regulations related to space tourism in order to encourage unhindered innovation within the industry.[16] This moratorium was set to expire in 2023, but even before then there was little the FAA could do to ensure the safety of space tourism aside from requiring that space tourism companies did not present a risk to the public on the ground. Those who engaged in space tourism until the moratorium expired and regulations were passed were outside of the government's control.

Additional points of contention in the space tourism industry include the environmental impact it has and what some perceive as a frivolous use of large amounts of money. Rockets emit CO_2 and soot in the atmosphere, which get trapped there and contribute to global warming.[17] Currently, about 100 rockets are launched each year, and Virgin Galactic alone anticipates that it will offer 400 spaceflights annually. This suggests a significant increase in rocket launches, and since each rocket emits 50 to 100 times as much CO_2 as a long-haul jet flight, this also suggests a large increase in CO_2 emissions.[18] Additionally, the sheer price of a ticket to space indicates that this is an experience that will be exclusively enjoyed by the wealthy, further contributing to tensions regarding income inequality. In the near future, short flights to space are anticipated to cost between $100,000 and $250,000, and though these prices are expected to decrease as the industry grows, prices are likely to continue to be prohibitively expensive to most individuals.[19]

Among the notable critics of the space tourism industry who have called it out as a frivolous waste of resources is the United

Kingdom's Prince William, who has argued that "we need some of the world's greatest brains and minds fixed on trying to repair this planet, not trying to find the next place to go and live."[20] However, proponents of space tourism argue that, as NASA's work has shown, space travel often offers the opportunity to learn more about Earth and its climate, and it's likely that privately owned space infrastructure will be used for this purpose as well. Furthermore, because these spaceflights will now be privately funded, there will be greater opportunity for innovation and discovery and space exploration. While government agencies like NASA have to be conservative in terms of financial and safety risks, private companies have more freedom to take risks, which could offer significant benefits in the fields of space exploration and Earth studies.[21]

Space militarization, tourism, and competition in both areas have been increasing since the mid-twentieth century, and recent developments such as the creation of the US Space Force and numerous competing space tourism companies suggest we are now at a turning point in these areas. Though the financial and environmental costs of space tourism and militarization are points of contention, the potential benefits for domestic security, economic growth, space exploration, and technological innovation offer arguments to support their ascent. The expert viewpoints provided in *Current Controversies: Space: Tourism, Competition, Militarization* offer readers the opportunity to better understand the nuanced perspectives on this complex issue.

Notes

1. Valerie Stimac, "A Definitive History of Space Tourism and Human Spaceflight," Space Tourism Guide, July 5, 2020, https://spacetourismguide.com/history-of-space-tourism/.
2. Adam Mann, "What Was the Space Race?" Space.com, August 7, 2019, https://www.space.com/space-race.html.
3. Jason Daley, "The US Military Has Been in Space from the Beginning," *Smithsonian Magazine*, June 19, 2018, https://www.smithsonianmag.com/smart-news/us-military-has-been-space-beginning-180969403/.

4. "NACA Overview," NASA, October 26, 2010, https://history.nasa.gov/naca/overview.html.

5. Jason Daley, "The US Military Has Been in Space from the Beginning," *Smithsonian Magazine*, June 19, 2018, https://www.smithsonianmag.com/smart-news/us-military-has-been-space-beginning-180969403/.

6. "Air Force Space Command History," United States Air Force, n.d., https://www.afspc.af.mil/About-Us/AFSPC-History/.

7. Bryan Bender, "What the Space Force Is, and Isn't," Politico, February 3, 2021, https://www.politico.com/news/2021/02/03/space-force-explained-465799.

8. "Treaty on Principles Governing the Activities of States in the Exploration and Use of Outer Space, Including the Moon and Other Celestial Bodies," United Nations Office for Disarmament Affairs, https://treaties.unoda.org/t/outer_space.

9. Loren Grush, "How an International Treaty Signed 50 Years Ago Became the Backbone for Space Law," the Verge, January 27, 2017, https://www.theverge.com/2017/1/27/14398492/outer-space-treaty-50-anniversary-exploration-guidelines.

10. Jill Stuart, "The Outer Space Treaty Has Been Remarkably Successful—but Is It Fit for the Modern Age?" the Conversation, January 27, 2017, https://theconversation.com/the-outer-space-treaty-has-been-remarkably-successful-but-is-it-fit-for-the-modern-age-71381.

11. Ibid.

12. Matt Weinzierl and Mehak Sarang, "The Commercial Space Age Is Here," *Harvard Business Review*, February 12, 2021, https://hbr.org/2021/02/the-commercial-space-age-is-here.

13. Francesca Street, "First Space Tourist Dennis Tito: 'It Was the Greatest Moment of My Life,'" CNN, July 20, 2021, https://www.cnn.com/travel/article/space-tourism-20-year-anniversary-scn/index.html.

14. Anri Ichimura, "The Big Three Space Tourism Companies, Compared," *Esquire*, July 16, 2021, https://www.esquiremag.ph/money/movers/biggest-space-tourism-companies-compared-a00304-20210716-lfrm.

15. Michael Sheetz, "Super Fast Travel Using Outer Space Could Be $20 Billion Market, Disrupting Airlines, UBS Predicts," CNBC, March 18, 2019, https://www.cnbc.com/2019/03/18/ubs-space-travel-and-space-tourism-a-23-billion-business-in-a-decade.html.

16. Tereza Pultarova, "Do Space Tourists Really Understand the Risk They're Taking?" Space.com, September 27, 2021, https://www.space.com/space-tourism-risk-safety-regulations.

17. Eloise Marais, "Space Tourism: Rockets Emit 100 Times More CO_2 Per Passenger Than Flights—Imagine a Whole Industry," the Conversation, July 19, 2021, https://theconversation.com/space-tourism-rockets-emit-100-times-more-co-per-passenger-than-flights-imagine-a-whole-industry-164601.

18. Ibid.

19. Jamie Carter, "Space Tourism Is Here: Booking a Trip to the Final Frontier," *Travel + Leisure*, September 1, 2021, https://www.travelandleisure.com/trip-ideas/space-astronomy/space-tourism-is-here.
20. George Bowden, "Prince William: Saving Earth Should Come Before Space Tourism," BBC News, October 14, 2021, https://www.bbc.com/news/uk-58903078.
21. Richard Hollingham, "Six Reasons Why Space Tourism Matters," BBC, April 7, 2014, https://www.bbc.com/future/article/20140408-six-reasons-space-tourism-matters.

Current Controversies

Chapter 1

Are Space Tourism and Private Space Travel Safe?

Overview: Space Technology Presents Many Opportunities and Challenges

Guglielmo S. Aglietti

Guglielmo S. Aglietti is a professor of mechanical engineering and head of the Space Institute at the University of Auckland in New Zealand. He consults with numerous companies in the UK space industry on various aspects of spacecraft structures and is a project principal investigator for RemoveDEBRIS, a project that demonstrates technologies for space debris removal.

With the launch of Sputnik in 1957 and the subsequent beginning of the space age, the progression of Space Technologies has, on the one hand, led to the development of hundreds of applications (Pelton et al., 2017) that use satellite data, including devices for everyday use, from satellite televisions to the Satnav in our cars. On the other, it has underpinned scientific progress in Earth and Atmospheric Sciences as well as in Astronomy and Astrophysics. Just to recall some of the highest public profile contributions from the field, satellite measurements showed the extent of the ozone layer depletion in the atmosphere and the existence of exoplanets and black holes have been confirmed, among many other scientific advances.

The rapid progress made in Space Technology led to extraordinary accomplishments for the whole human race, such as the Moon landing.

At the same time, these space missions have provided powerful iconic imagery for humanity, and photos like the Blue Marble (Wuebbles, 2012) have become universally recognized symbols of our planet and its extraordinary environment and finite resources.

Although the spectacular progress in Space Technologies slowed down toward the end of the past century, together with that of the whole Aerospace sector, very important achievements continued to be made. These include the development of the International Space Station and the robotic exploration of other planets and celestial bodies, including landing on a comet!

Through the years, space has often been identified as the new frontier, fueling the imagination of writers and film directors, who created visions (more or less plausible) of a future enabled by fantastic developments in Space Technologies.

However, consistent with what history has shown us, is the fact that, after an initial phase of "exploration" of a new environment and consolidation of the relevant technologies, what follows is an explosion of businesses to exploit the new opportunities offered by the new environment. This is where we are today. Sometimes called Space 4.0, we are in a period that has seen a shift of paradigms, with changes of motivations, actors, and, indeed, technologies (PWC Report, 2019).

New Space and the Need for Appropriate Regulatory Framework

Under the name of "New Space,"[1] there is an ongoing "revolution" in the space sector with new players/commercial entrepreneurs/ businesses (Hall, 2020) entering a domain traditionally occupied by institutional players ("Old Space," e.g., space agencies working with large companies) to exploit the new opportunities opening in front of them. These could include new services, offered through applications of space data (from precision navigation/agriculture, surveillance, to Earth environment monitoring, etc.), to more futuristic opportunities, such as space tourism or asteroid mining. Successful entrepreneurs from other sectors, from Richard Branson in the UK to Elon Musk in the US, have entered the "space" arena, taking risks and challenging the conservativism of the established "Old Space" business model.

Here is where we can identify a first challenge and learn a lesson from history, preventing space from becoming a lawless "wild west" where the strongest can take an unfair advantage. This should apply to Low Earth Orbit (LEO), where the current regulatory framework should be further developed and enforced to manage the increasing "space traffic" (Cukurtepe and Akgun, 2009; Lal et al., 2018) (to prevent interferences or collisions between assets of different operators), as well as to Medium (MEO) or Geosynchronous Earth Orbit (GEO) and interplanetary exploration and exploitation. Indeed, new regulations should be implemented respecting established treaties and principles (e.g., "Outer Space Treaty" or the "Convention on International Liability for Damage Caused by Space Objects").

In areas where an appropriate regulatory framework is already in operation and largely followed by all the stakeholders, like the satellite telecommunication sector (ITU, 2012), the challenge becomes to stay abreast with technology progress and market evolution (Morozova and Vasyanin, 2019). Together with the challenge, there is an opportunity to develop new regulations that spur further technological progress.

The issue of the overcrowded radio-frequency spectrum, as well as the sustainability of the space environment, which is threatened by the growing amount of space debris, have to be tackled. Solutions that are acceptable to the various stakeholders (from commercial organizations to political entities) have to be found and, most importantly, implemented.

Activities in space cannot be contained within the boundary of a country's border and have the potential to affect assets or areas of the planet well-beyond the jurisdiction of a launching country or the nation where a satellite operator is registered. Therefore, the international regulatory framework should clearly prevail on national regulations and limit the capability of countries to use less stringent regulations as a means to attract foreign business. At the same time, some consideration also has to be given to how to enforce at an international level the agreed rules and regulations.

Indeed, the development of rules and regulations must be mitigated to avoid unnecessary red tape stifling new enterprises, and space law should preserve the freedom to generate new ideas and implement new applications. Hence the challenge lies in balancing these competing requirements: a regulatory framework that protects stakeholders, countries' interests, and current and future human rights on one side, with the freedom to develop and exploit new technologies on the other.

Technical Challenges

Propulsion Systems

Coming now to the more technical challenges, propulsion systems performance is a significant hurdle to overcome in the space sector (Turner et al., 2009).

Starting with the launch vehicles, their capabilities (broadly speaking, payload size, and thrust) have essentially plateaued, as only relatively minor incremental progress has been made in the last decades. Indeed, materials have improved with the introduction of composites with mechanical properties far superior to the typical alloys that were used at the beginning of the space age. Design and manufacturing techniques have also improved, with progress in software simulation enabled by the extraordinary growth of computer power, or new manufacturing methods such as additive manufacturing. Guidance and control systems have also improved thanks to advances in electronics and software. However, besides the push toward green propellants (Gohardani et al., 2014), nothing substantial has changed with the solid or liquid propellants performance and related technologies, which are key to overall launcher capability (Devezas, 2018). Reusable launchers are being used by a few companies in order to reduce costs or increase launch frequencies, and it is undeniable that costs have slowly come down, although this is largely due to combinations of countries' policies and market forces, but truly economic access to space is yet to be achieved.

On a longer timescale, the challenge is to develop and implement technologies, such as hypersonic air breathing rocket engines,[2] to be used in hybrid launchers to cut the need for large amounts of oxygen that have to be carried by current vehicles. Launch vehicles that could take off and land as aircraft, without the need for extensive and expensive service between missions, should also be developed. Similarly, in-space propulsion offers opportunities for improvement, in particular on electric propulsion systems, which are also hybrid systems that would utilize different modes of operation (Levchenko et al., 2020).

Propulsion systems performance are also fundamental to interplanetary missions in terms of enabling faster travel and larger payloads to be delivered where required. Our current limitations in the manned exploration of the solar system are mainly due to the length of travel, which is directly related to the level of performance that is available from existing propulsion systems. Similarly, propulsion systems performance limits our exploration and exploitation capabilities (also for robotic activities) as it is a significant limitation to the mass of payload that can be safely transported to/from other celestial bodies.

Protection of Humans

Strictly related to human exploration are space health and medicine (Hodkinson et al., 2017), to enable humans to withstand the space environment for long periods, and the creation of artificial habitats in space and on other planets to support a reasonable quality of human life. The challenge here consists in the creation of a whole artificial environment to support people's well-being and physical and mental health, with means protecting against the negative effects of the space environment (Grimm, 2019). Whether we are considering a man-made vessel for long distance space travel or a space platform for large-scale human inhabitation or a planetary colony, some challenges overlap. These overlapping challenges include the need to create efficient closed loop systems to replenish resources and minimize waste, with the common goal to generate an artificial ecosystem for the long-term support of human life.[3]

Another aspect of our need to protect and preserve human life is the issue of planetary defense (Simpson, 2015).

Near Earth Objects like asteroids or comets can pose a significant threat. Although smaller objects (such as meteors) hit our planet daily and mostly burn up whilst traveling though the atmosphere, some larger objects can survive and hit the Earth's surface with significant energy. Most of the craters produced by the larger objects that have hit Earth since its formation have been erased by the planets geological processes, but there are dozens of large craters still visible (a great example is the 1 kilometer wide Barringer Meteor Crater in Arizona, which was formed ~50,000 years ago by the impact of a metallic object ~50 m in diameter) that serve as reminders that these impacts can occur. Depending on the size of the object, which could be 100s of meters or kilometers in diameter, and the location of the impact, consequences could range from relatively minor damage, to a major catastrophe that could destroy life on vast regions of the planet, if not all life entirely. Fortunately, the probability of these events is very low, but their consequences are dramatic, hence appropriate mitigation strategies must be developed. All major space organizations (NASA, ESA, etc.) have given some attention to this issue (Office of Audits, 2014) (ESA Asteroid Impact Mission [AIM] and NASA Double Asteroid Redirection Test [DART]), and the United Nations have taken good steps to improve coordination, establishing the International Asteroid Warning Network and the Space Mission Planning Advisory Group (SMPAG). However, as this is a global threat, a greater level of international coordination and integration of the efforts made by single entities is necessary to produce an effective response. Should the threat of catastrophic impact from a large asteroid materialize, the world cannot afford a disorderly and fragmented response, such as that seen with past global crises (e.g., the Covid-19 pandemic). Time will be limited so the plans have to be prepared and agreed upon, ready to be executed in order to produce a timely response and perform the necessary mission.

From a technical perspective, besides the challenges to improve detection capabilities and potential impact predictions, the development and testing of methodologies and technologies to deflect a large object (as this currently seems the most realistic and effective method of intervention) have to progress to the point that it could be deployed with a high level of confidence in its success.

Earth Environment

Following the theme of the protection of the Earth, climate change is a significant threat to our environment with potentially disastrous consequences, and is an area where Satellite Technologies can help in tackling the challenge (Brünner et al., 2018). On a global scale, satellites provide impartial information to monitor the environment and develop and validate models improving our predictive capabilities. But greater effort has to be placed in producing actionable information related to specific needs and issues, reducing the vast amount of data to simpler interpretations that can inform the political discourse.

Both institutional and private Earth Observation (EO) markets demand very high resolution and coverage, as well as a short revisit time, with the aim to achieve real time Earth Observation. From surveillance to disaster monitoring and management of resources, there are literally hundreds of applications, but still there is a relatively low market adoption. This becomes obvious if we compare satellite EO with satellite telecommunications, as in the latter sector there is an abundance of purely commercial organizations that operate (without institutional support) in a user-driven market, whereas the

EO market is still most often enabled by institutional budgets. There is a clear trend toward a more commercial EO sector that is facilitated by smaller sized and cheaper satellites (Rycroft and Crosby, 2013), and several companies offering cost effective solutions promising technically acceptable performance at a price that the market can bear. However, there is very high competition in a market that still has too small a number of customers.

Low Cost Space Technologies

This democratization and marketization of space is evident in the growth of the cubesat market (Davoli et al., 2019). Here, space HW is available at prices so low that it has attracted a growing number of customers (from Space Agencies to institutions like universities and schools), which in turn have enabled the creation of start-ups and spinoffs. However, the performance of these systems are very limited, and often the constraints come from their physical size (e.g., the size of the optics limits the resolution that can be achieved, or the size of the solar panels limits the amount of power that can be collected). This has led to the development of deployable structures to package relevant elements into small (cubesat compatible) volumes and then deploy them in space to achieve the required level of performance. Sometime these act as demonstrations for applications aimed at larger satellites, like drag sails (Underwood et al., 2019).

There are other technical issues that affect all smaller mass satellites, not just cubesats, and present significant challenges, like the need to achieve high platform stability. This is crucial for all missions supporting highly accurately targeted optical payloads (e.g., high-resolution cameras/telescopes or laser communication systems) or devices that demand stability for inertial types of measurements. The issue lies with the minimization of the micro-vibrations that are produced by essential on-board equipment (Remedia et al., 2015), and that can, for example, produce unacceptable oscillations of the line of sight. This issue is more severe for smaller craft as there is less mass (inertia), which naturally reduces the vibration level. Ground testing and modeling to predict in-orbit performance are still inaccurate and practical applications rely on the use of large margins rather than accurate models. Active control of micro-vibrations is still very difficult and too expensive to be implemented, in particular at the lower end of the market, where most growth is expected.

In terms of their overall performance, cubesat capabilities are often oversold to an inexperienced public, and there is a general need for higher quality products with the involved hardware that still maintain affordability.

Large Space Structures

At the other end of the spectrum, with respect to cubesats, in terms of size, are Large Space Structures (LSS). These have been considered and studied for decades, but real progress has been slow.

The capability to deploy LSS is another factor that, similarly to advances in propulsion, would enable a range of applications, but they present a series of significant challenges that depend on the specific areas.

On the one hand there are instruments like telescopes, cameras, and antennas that require large (>10 m and possibly an order of magnitude larger) high-precision reflective surfaces. Here the current methodologies (e.g., based on the deployment of precisely machined and polished mirrors whose positions and shape can be adjusted by a series of actuators) are limited by the size and number of segments that can be deployed (e.g., James Webb Space Telescope [JWST]),[4] and the overall staggering cost. Concerning the antennas, a variety of deployable solutions have been proposed, from inflatables to tensegrity structures, but Europe still needs to develop an appropriate commercial solution for current and future applications. Overall, new lighter-weight technologies have to be deployed, to increase packaging efficiency without compromising the quality of the final reflector.

On the other hand, there are future applications like Satellite Solar Power[5] where the sheer size of the structure (square kilometers) is the challenge, rather than the geometrical precision that must be achieved by the assembled structure. Extreme light weight and packaging efficiency have to be achieved, as well as in-orbit deployment and assembly capabilities that are beyond the state of the art.

In-Orbit Servicing and Active Debris Removal

This brings us to the opportunities offered by robotic in-orbit servicing and the development of flexible technologies that can support multipurpose missions. These opportunities include the servicing and potential repairing of current satellites, to active debris removal. These are not new concepts, as in 1984 the Space Shuttle *Discovery* mission STS-51-A brought back to Earth two old satellites no longer functioning (probably the first example of Active Debris Removal), and similarly the mission of the shuttle *Endeavor* in 1993 (and other following missions) provided essential fixes and services to the Hubble Space Telescope. However, the opportunity here is to develop robotic technologies (Wilde et al., 2019) able to perform these type of missions (Forshaw et al., 2016) at a fraction of the cost. The non-cooperative nature of the target, which could be tumbling, presents the first challenge to any approaching vehicle that has to rendezvous with this object. Techniques to stabilize the target and devices to safely grasp it have to be developed (and standardized) as well as improvements made in the relative navigation (vision-based navigation), hardware, and software. Some progress has been made and some devices tested in-orbit (Aglietti et al., 2020), but we are still far from a real capability to perform Active Debris Removal or in-orbit servicing with sufficient confidence and at an affordable price.

This article has described some of the challenges that the space sector is facing, but there are more, and these come with opportunities for new developments (for example, those offered by multifunctional space structures (Sairajan et al., 2016), or technologies like optical and quantum intersatellite communication (Liao et al., 2017). The solutions to the various issues, which in time will be developed, will provide stepping stones for future applications and enterprises that will benefit societies across the world.

Footnotes

1. https://en.wikipedia.org/wiki/NewSpace (accessed March 4, 2020)
2. https://en.wikipedia.org/wiki/SABRE_(rocket_engine)
3. https://www.nasa.gov/content/life-support-systems
4. https://www.jwst.nasa.gov/content/observatory/ote/mirrors/index.html
5. Solar power satellites DM Flournoy, Springer, 2011

Over 50 Years of Research Has Helped Scientists Understand Space Travel's Effect on the Human Body

Laurie J. Abadie, Nathan Cranford, Charles W. Lloyd, Mark J. Shelhamer, and Jennifer L. Turner

Laurie J. Abadie is the lead for Artemis Initial Capabilities in NASA's Human Research Program. Nathan Cranford is a science writer and communications strategist who works with the NASA Johnson Space Center. Charles W. Lloyd is a manager of NASA's Human Research Program. Mark J. Shelhamer is a human spaceflight researcher and former chief scientist of NASA's Human Research Program. Jennifer L. Turner is a CRONUS flight controller for the International Space Station.

For over 50 years, NASA's Human Research Program (HRP) has studied what happens to the human body in space. Researchers are using what they learn to design procedures, devices, and strategies to keep astronauts safe and healthy throughout their missions.

NASA engineers use the lessons learned to better design spacecraft and improve the fit and functions of spacesuits. The research also aids in the development and assessment of medical standards, physical fitness programs and standards, physiological and psychological adaptation training, sensorimotor training, and nutritional health protocols.

Understanding the effects of spaceflight on humans is essential as astronauts move from the International Space Station in low-Earth orbit to deep space destinations on and around the Moon, and beyond. With the Artemis program, NASA will land the first woman and next man on the Moon using innovative technologies

"The Human Body in Space," by Laurie J. Abadie, Nathan Cranford, Charles W. Lloyd, Mark J. Shelhamer, and Jennifer L. Turner, NASA, February 2, 2021.

to explore more of the lunar surface than ever before, gathering new data while keeping astronauts healthy and safe.

NASA is particularly interested in investigating how the body reacts to long-duration spaceflight as the agency plans for extended missions on the Moon and Mars. Scott Kelly and Christina Koch were the first American astronauts to spend nearly one year in space onboard the space station, twice the previous average. Scott, Christina, and six other astronauts have spent more than 200 days in space during a single spaceflight.

In addition to spending almost a year in space, Scott was involved in the unique Twins Study. Scott participated in several biomedical studies onboard the space station while his identical twin brother, retired astronaut Mark Kelly, stayed on Earth as a control subject, someone who provides a basis of comparison. The study provided valuable data about what happened to Scott, physiologically and psychologically, as compared to his brother Mark. Their contribution to science helped generate data that researchers will use for decades to come.

NASA is planning more dedicated extended-duration research on the space station. The studies are expected to shed light on how the body adapts to living in the spaceflight environment for various longer time periods, which will be pivotal for future deep space missions.

What exactly happens to the body in space and what are the risks? Are the risks the same for astronauts who spend six months on the space station versus those who may be away on a Mars mission for years? The simple answer is "no." NASA is researching risks for Mars missions which are grouped into five human spaceflight hazards related to the stressors they place on the body. These can be summarized with the acronym "RIDGE," short for Space Radiation, Isolation and Confinement, Distance from Earth, Gravity Fields, and Hostile/Closed Environments.

1. Space Radiation

On Earth, we are shielded by the planet's magnetic field and atmosphere from the majority of particles that make up the space radiation environment. Even so, everyone on Earth is exposed to low levels of radiation every day, from the food we eat to the air we breathe. In space, astronauts are exposed to varied and increased levels of radiation that are different from those on Earth. Three major sources contribute to the space radiation environment: particles trapped in Earth's magnetic field, solar energetic particles from the Sun, and galactic cosmic rays. A big challenge in reducing the risks of radiation exposure is that some space radiation particles (especially galactic cosmic rays) are difficult to shield against. Exposure to increased radiation can be associated with both short- and long-term health consequences, depending on how much total radiation astronauts experience and the time frame in which they experience that exposure. Increased risk of cancer and degenerative diseases, such as heart disease and cataracts, have been observed in human populations exposed to radiation on Earth. Health risks for astronauts from radiation exposure in space are mainly driven by long-term impacts. Additionally, animal and cellular research indicate that the type of radiation in the space environment has a larger impact on health outcomes compared to the radiation experienced on Earth. Not only will astronauts be exposed to more radiation in space than on Earth, but the radiation they are exposed to could pose increased risks.

The Key: The current strategy to reduce the health risks of space radiation exposure is to implement shielding, radiation monitoring, and specific operational procedures. Compared to typical six-month space station missions, later Moon and Mars missions will be much longer on average. Consequently, the total amount of radiation experienced and associated health risks may increase. NASA is developing new radiation detectors to monitor and characterize the radiation environment, which will provide better estimates of the dose and type of radiation to which the crews are exposed. Scientists and engineers are optimizing and implementing operational procedures that use available vehicle stowage and materials to reduce radiation exposure effectively. To investigate the health risks of space radiation exposure beyond low-

Earth orbit, NASA supports research that analyzes the biological effects of simulated cosmic rays at ground-based research facilities. Research at these facilities helps NASA understand and reduce the risk of space radiation, ensure proper measurement of the doses that astronauts receive on the space station and in future spacecraft, and develop advanced materials that improve radiation shielding for future missions. Studies of radiation-exposed human cohorts are also being conducted to estimate the health risks in populations relevant to astronauts.

2. Isolation and Confinement

Expedition crews selected for a stay onboard the space station are carefully chosen, trained, and supported to ensure they will be able to work effectively as a team for the duration of their six to 12-month missions. Crews for a Moon or Mars mission will undergo even more careful assessment, selection, and preparation since they will travel farther and potentially for longer than previous humans in an isolated and confined environment, with only a few other people. Additionally, crews will likely be international and multi-cultural, making cross-cultural sensitivity and team dynamics paramount to mission success. Ensuring astronauts get quality sleep is also important; otherwise, their internal biological clocks, or circadian rhythm, might be altered by factors like different dark and light cycles, a small and noisy environment, the stress of prolonged isolation and confinement, and a 37-minute extended day on Mars. It is important to prepare for the fatigue astronauts may experience during spaceflight, given that there will be times with heavy workloads and shifting schedules. To prevent crew boredom, NASA considers the kinds of activities in which the astronauts will participate during a multi-year round trip to Mars. Communication and understanding among crew members are vital to the success of the mission, and changes in morale and motivation are possible as the mission unfolds. This may relate to reduced stimulation, the longing for loved ones, or feeling unable to assist with family emergencies back on Earth, regardless of how long the mission lasts. Using spaceflight analogs on Earth, NASA's research has revealed that both the duration and type of confined and isolated experience are important to consider. The more restricted the space, and the less contact with people outside the environment, the more likely humans are to develop behavioral or cognitive conditions or psychiatric disorders.

The Key: NASA has been studying people in isolated and confined environments for years, and has developed methods and technologies to counteract possible problems. NASA scientists are using devices, such as actigraphy, that help assess and improve sleep and alertness by recording how much people move and how much ambient light is around them. New lighting, spurred by the development of Light-Emitting Diode (LED) technology, is used on the space station to help align astronaut's circadian rhythms and to improve sleep, alertness, and performance. A 10-minute self-test of vigilance and attention assesses the effect of fatigue on performance. Astronauts write in journals as a safe place to vent frustrations and provide researchers a tool to study behavioral issues that are on the minds of crew members who are living and working in isolation and confinement. Researchers are also looking into using virtual reality to simulate relaxing environments to help improve the mood of crews in isolation. Engaging in relevant, meaningful activities, including learning a language or learning new medical skills, could help ward off depression and boost morale. Crews may even tend to a space garden, which could have positive behavioral health benefits in addition to providing a fresh source of food and helping to purify the air. Researchers are using Earth-based analogs to investigate how much privacy and living space will be needed on longer missions where crew members will be restricted in a relatively small spacecraft together. NASA is also determining strategies to formulate the best crew by studying individual and team attributes, composition, and dynamics.

3. Distance from Earth

The space station orbits 240 miles above Earth. The Moon is 1,000 times farther from Earth than the space station. In contrast, Mars is on average 140 million miles from Earth. With a communication delay of up to 20 minutes one-way while on Mars, astronauts must be able to solve problems and identify solutions as a team without help from NASA's mission control. The types of food and medicine to be packed for a multi-year trip without access to a grocery store or pharmacy are also important to consider. Unlike space station crews, which regularly receive supplies from cargo flights from Earth, astronauts going to Mars will have to bring all of the food, equipment, and medical supplies they need.

The Key: NASA is using its human spaceflight experience on the space station to figure out what types of medical events happen in space over time and what types of skills, procedures, equipment, and supplies are needed so that they will have a good idea of what to pack for future missions to the Moon and Mars. Space station astronauts already receive medical training before and during space missions that teach them how to respond to health problems as they arise. For example, astronauts learn how to use onboard space station equipment to produce an intravenous (IV) solution from purified water, which can be used for medical administration. Crew members also perform ultrasound scans on each other to monitor organ health. If one crew member becomes sick during the mission, crews are ready to perform laboratory testing to help make the right diagnosis and guide treatment. NASA is working on developing a medical data architecture for spacecraft that enables the capabilities of clinical decision support tools, which could use artificial intelligence and machine learning to further help diagnose and treat various illnesses. Researchers are also looking into the role that virtual assistants could play to help crews identify and respond to spaceflight anomalies quickly for more distant missions. Additionally, the agency is studying and improving food formulation, processing, packaging, and preservation systems to ensure the nutrients remain stable and the food remains acceptable for years. Space-resilient medications and packaging systems that preserve the integrity of pharmaceuticals for long-duration missions are another significant part of NASA's research.

4. Gravity Fields

Astronauts will encounter three different gravity fields on a Mars mission. On the six-month trek between the planets, crews will be weightless. While living and working on Mars, crews will be in approximately one-third of Earth's gravity. Finally upon returning home, crews will have to readapt to Earth's gravity. Transitioning from one gravity field to another is trickier than it sounds. It affects spatial orientation, head-eye and hand-eye coordination, balance, and locomotion, with some crew members experiencing space motion sickness. Landing a spacecraft on Mars could be challenging as astronauts adjust to the gravity field of another celestial body. When shifting from weightlessness to gravity, astronauts may experience post-flight orthostatic intolerance where they are unable to maintain their blood pressure when standing up, which can lead to lightheadedness and fainting. NASA has learned that without Earth's gravity affecting the human body, weight-bearing bones lose on average 1% to 1.5% of mineral density per month during spaceflight. After returning to Earth, bone loss might not be completely corrected by rehabilitation; however, their risk for fracture is not higher. Without the proper diet and exercise routine, astronauts also lose muscle mass in microgravity faster than they would on Earth. Moreover, the fluids in the body shift upward to the head in microgravity, which may put pressure on the eyes and cause vision problems. If preventive or countermeasures are not implemented, crews may experience an increased risk of developing kidney stones due to dehydration and increased excretion of calcium from their bones.

The Key: By analyzing how the body changes in weightlessness and after returning to Earth's gravity, NASA is developing protective measures against these changes for a Mars mission. Functional task testing is in place to help detect and improve balance control after landing on a gravitational surface. Fine motor skills testing is done to detect any changes in the ability of astronauts to interact with computer-based devices. Distribution of the fluids in the body is closely monitored to help evaluate any connection to changes in vision. Compression cuffs worn on the thighs help keep the blood in the lower extremities to counteract those fluid shifts. A lower-body negative pressure device could help draw fluids from the head into the legs as well. Back pain, which some astronauts have reported experiencing during spaceflight, is monitored by obtaining spinal ultrasounds. Muscle size and bone density are assessed for deterioration using MRI and high-resolution imaging techniques, before and after flight. Crew members perform periodic fitness self-evaluations to help researchers better understand the decline in heart function that can occur during spaceflight. Medicines that NASA is studying, such as potassium citrate, may help combat the physiological change that could increase the risk of developing kidney stones. Bisphosphonate medications have been shown in NASA studies to be effective in preventing bone loss. NASA has also designed an efficient way to collect and measure how much urine a crew member produces in space, which is essential to human research since it reveals key information about a person's health. For example, researchers can analyze different levels of certain substances in an astronaut's urine to determine whether they are at risk of developing a kidney stone in space, and make modifications to the diet, exercise routine, and water intake as preventive measures. Aerobic and resistive exercise has been shown to keep the heart healthy, bones and muscles strong, the mind alert, as well as maintain a more positive outlook, and may even help with balance and coordination. Software-generated workout partners could be used to help motivate astronauts to exercise regularly for longer space missions. NASA has even completed a joint Earth-based bed rest study to determine whether centrifuge artificial gravity may be an effective way to counter the physiological effects of weightlessness.

5. Hostile/Closed Environments

NASA has learned that the ecosystem inside the spacecraft plays a big role in everyday astronaut life in space. Microbes can change characteristics in space, and micro-organisms that naturally live on the human body are transferred more easily from person to person in closed habitats, such as the space station. Stress hormone levels are elevated and the immune system is altered, which could lead to increased susceptibility to allergies or other illnesses. Earth-based analogs do not perfectly simulate the spaceflight environment, making them insufficient for studying on the ground how human immune systems react in space. However, NASA-funded Antarctic analog studies could provide insight into how certain spaceflight stressors may affect the human immune system. What is known is that spaceflight changes the immune system, although crews do not tend to get sick upon returning to Earth. Even though astronauts' acquired immunity is intact, more research is needed into whether spaceflight induced altered immunity may lead to autoimmune issues, in which the immune system mistakenly attacks the healthy cells, organs, and tissues present in the body. Beyond the effects of the environment on the immune system, every inch and detail of living and working quarters must be carefully thought-out and designed. No one wants their house to be too hot, too cold, cramped, crowded, loud, or not well lit, and no one would enjoy working and living in such a habitat in space either.

The Key: NASA is using technology to monitor the air quality of the space station to ensure the atmosphere is safe to breathe and not contaminated with gases, such as formaldehyde, ammonia, and carbon monoxide. Thermal Control Systems function to maintain temperatures of the space station and keep astronauts comfortable. Blood and saliva samples are analyzed to identify changes in the immune system and the reactivation of latent viruses during spaceflight. NASA uses advanced molecular techniques to evaluate the risk of microbes that may cause illness for crew members. Various parts of the body and the space station are swabbed regularly for analysis of the microbial population that inhabits the environment. Crews change out air filters, clean surfaces, and treat the water to prevent illnesses that may result from the accumulation of contaminants. Astronauts are advised to get a flu shot to boost their immunity and are quarantined before their missions to avoid catching any sort of illness before launch. During the Twins Study and One-Year Mission, Scott Kelly administered a flu vaccine to himself while his brother received his on Earth. The immunization proved to work as well in space as it does on Earth, which is a good finding for longer missions to the Moon and Mars. Living quarters and work environments are carefully planned and evaluated to ensure that designs balance comfort and efficiency. Lighting onboard the space station is similar to what would be experienced naturally on Earth, thanks to the new LED lighting system.

NASA is taking action on all of these risks and working to solve the challenges of human spaceflight with some of the most brilliant minds in their fields. The results garnered from laboratories, ground analogs, and space station missions will provide more insight into these adaptations and present a stepping stone for longer missions. On upcoming Artemis missions to lunar orbit and the surface of the Moon, even more data will be collected as this work continues. On future longer duration missions to the Moon and Mars, astronauts will benefit from years of research that will ensure they will be able not just to survive, but thrive on their spacefaring missions.

High-Profile Accidents in Space Travel Lead to Improved Safety and Regulatory Standards

Hamza Bendemra

Hamza Bendemra is a machine learning engineer who writes for Towards Data Science. He previously served as a research fellow with the Aerospace Research and Innovation Centre (ARIC) at Khalifa University in Abu Dhabi, UAE.

Last week was a particularly grim one for private space flights. Virgin Galactic's SpaceShipTwo crashed in the Mojave Desert, about 150 km north of Los Angeles, killing a pilot, Michael Alsbury, and seriously injuring another, Peter Siebold.

Although the US National Transportation Safety Board investigation is ongoing, there have been reports the "feathering" system that SpaceShipTwo uses may have been prematurely activated, leading to the crash.

Earlier in the week, an unmanned Antares rocket, taking cargo to the International Space Station, exploded shortly after take-off.

Space travel is a risky business. As we push for technological advances and further exploration, accidents unfortunately happen. Spacecraft are extremely complicated systems, with countless aspects to consider, simulate and test to ensure successful take-off and re-entry.

Here are five key space accidents that have defined modern space travel, and the reasons they happened.

1. Voskhod 2: March 19, 1965

Failure: equipment malfunction during re-entry.

The Russian Voskhod 2 mission is best known as it was the first successful spacewalk in history. The spacecraft had two

"Five Space Travel Accidents That Shaped the Modern Era," by Hamza Bendemra, The Conversation, November 5, 2014. https://theconversation.com/five-space-travel-accidents-that-shaped-the-modern-era-33759.

crew members on board: Pavel Belyayev and Alexey Leonov. Leonov was the first person to leave a spacecraft to conduct a 12-minute spacewalk.

However, it had a disastrous re-entry in which a malfunction of the automatic landing system forced the pilots to land the spacecraft manually, in a heavily forested area located more than 300 km (186 miles) away from the intended landing zone. Leonov and Belyayev survived, but their mission control did not know their locations. After spending a night in freezing temperatures, they were finally spotted and rescued.

2. Soyuz 1: April 24, 1967

Failure: parachute failure during re-entry.

Soyuz 1 was launched carrying astronaut Colonel Vladimir Komarov. Upon re-entry, Komarov died after his module crashed when both the main chute and back-up parachutes failed to open.

His death was particularly controversial due to the numerous system failures in previous tests reported by engineers, but ignored by the Soviet establishment.

The mission was plagued with other problems, including a faulty solar panel. The tragedy resulted in an 18-month delay in the subsequent launches of Soyuz 2 and Soyuz 3, but led to improvements in the program.

3. Soyuz 11: June 30, 1971

Failure: decompression in capsule during re-entry.

Russian Soyuz 11 is known for boarding Salyut 1, the first space station, but the mission ended tragically when the crew capsule depressurised during re-entry, asphyxiating all three crew members.

The culprit was a breathing ventilation valve that opened during re-entry, allowing oxygen in the capsule to escape. The crew were not wearing spacesuits. Following the accident, the Soyuz spacecraft was redesigned to allow astronauts to wear spacesuits during launch and landing.

4. Space Shuttle Challenger: January 28, 1986

Failure: mechanical failure during take-off.

As the crew of the Space Shuttle Challenger began their ascent, the shuttle suddenly broke apart 73 seconds into its flight and burst into flames, killing seven crew members. The source of the explosion was found to be an O-ring—a seal placed in solid rocket boosters used during take-off—that failed and led to the explosion.

A special commission appointed by Ronald Reagan to investigate the accident found NASA had disregarded warnings from engineers that the use of the O-rings in the low-temperature conditions on the morning of the launch presented a danger.

5. Space Shuttle Columbia: February 1, 2003

Failure: disintegration upon re-entry.

Space Shuttle Columbia suddenly disintegrated as it was descending towards the Kennedy Space Centre, resulting in the death of all seven astronauts, and several thousands of pieces of debris landing across Texas and Louisiana.

The tragic accident was caused by a piece of foam insulation that broke off and hit the left wing. The damage allowed hot gases to penetrate and destroy the internal wing structure upon re-entry, slowly breaking apart the aircraft. The disaster led to several changes including adding on-orbit inspections, and the preparation of a rescue mission if irreparable damage is found.

Is the Era of Space Tourism Over Before It Even Started?

Each of these five disasters resulted in changes that contributed to making space travel safer for the subsequent space missions—albeit the price can be measured in human lives.

As pointed out by Fredrick Jenet on The Conversation yesterday, failure is a necessary part of great success, as shown by the 55 mission failures and only 41 that led to space missions to the moon. Unfortunately, catastrophic failure in aviation can result in loss of life.

Virgin Galactic has been at the forefront of space tourism with their innovative SpaceShipTwo aircraft, with Richard Branson booked on-board on an inaugural flight in the next few months and commercial service expected to begin early next year. It is now unclear how long it will take for Virgin Galactic to offer space travel to the public.

The tragic accident is unlikely to result in the end of space tourism as major space companies continue to grow and move forward. History shows new regulations and safety procedures are likely to result from the investigation, leading to safer space travel in the future.

Though Congress Is Considering Regulations, Commercial Space Travel Currently Lacks Sufficient Regulation

Alyssa K. King

Alyssa K. King is a capture manager of global business and government affairs with SpaceX. She previously served as a commercial space transportation policy analyst with the Congressional Research Service.

Companies in the United States are advancing plans to offer paying customers rides into space on a regular basis. This development has been encouraged by Congress, which passed legislation in 2004 meant to enable commercial space transportation companies to develop business models under relatively light regulation.[1] While this approach has contributed to rapid growth in commercial launches of private satellites and of government cargoes, it has created uncertainty with respect to passenger transportation, as a nascent industry awaits guidance about what measures the government will require to keep paying passengers safe not only in space but on the way there and back to Earth.

A space tourism boom has been forecast for more than a decade,[2] but the current regulatory landscape is designed for a fledgling industry that is yet to fully emerge.[3] Companies proposing to offer space tourism, which have stayed afloat financially with the help of investors who foresee long-term opportunities, will at least initially be dependent on a limited pool of exceptionally wealthy customers.[4] When and to what extent it should be regulated by the government remain undecided.

This report provides an overview of the commercial space tourism industry and examines current federal safety standards for human spaceflight, opportunities for development of oversight

"The Future of Space Tourism," by Alyssa K. King, Congressional Research Service, August 28, 2020. Reprinted by permission.

frameworks, industry recommendations, medical considerations for space travelers, and other regulatory issues Congress may face as space transportation companies begin flying and accommodating paying customers.

[...]

Regulating Space Tourism

The U.S. government currently has no procedures for certifying the safety of launch vehicles or space travel for tourists. An exhaustive certification process exists for commercial spacecraft transporting NASA astronauts, but the same standards have not been formally required of space vehicles for tourist use.[25]

Federal law defines a spaceflight participant as "an individual, who is not crew or a government astronaut, carried within a launch vehicle or reentry vehicle."[26] The few existing regulations pertaining to commercial spaceflight participant safety address the responsibility of a launch provider to inform a spaceflight passenger of certain risks and of the vehicle's safety track record.[27] There are currently no federal rules related to suborbital operations or to the operation of privately owned space stations and private vehicles in space. Federal regulations related to space vehicle reentry pertain principally to the safety of people on the ground, not to the safety of passengers or crew members aboard commercial spaceflights.

Federal Aviation Administration Oversight Responsibilities

The Commercial Space Launch Amendments Act of 2004 (CSLAA; P.L. 108-492) designated FAA as the regulatory authority for oversight and licensing of commercial space launch activities. FAA's Office of Commercial Space Transportation issued rules in 2006 setting requirements for crew and participants aboard commercial flights.[28] Unless FAA has issued paying spaceflight participants their own licenses to launch and operate a spacecraft, an FAA-licensed crew is required on board any vehicle launched from the United States that is carrying passengers in space.

Under the human spaceflight requirements, the crew aboard a commercial space vehicle must be trained to carry out duties on the ground or onboard so the space vehicle does not harm the public. This training includes abort scenarios and emergency operations. Additionally, the crew must demonstrate an ability to withstand the stressors of spaceflight. Each crew member with a safety-critical role must possess a current FAA second-class airman medical certificate.[29]

FAA requires that a space vehicle operator must inform any spaceflight participant in writing of the risks associated with launch and reentry and provide the safety record of the launch vehicle prior to accepting compensation or making an agreement to fly a paying customer.[30]

During the informed consent process, an operator must present the risks in a "manner that can be readily understood" by spaceflight participants without specialized education or training. The vehicle operator must obtain a consent letter from each flight participant accepting the risks after the operator provides the following in writing:

- each known hazard that could result in serious injury or death;
- acknowledgement that there are unknown hazards;
- a disclaimer that participation in spaceflight may result in death, serious injury, or total or partial loss of physical or mental function;
- a disclaimer that the U.S. government has not certified the launch vehicle as safe for carrying crew or passengers; and
- a description of the vehicle's safety record, to include any accidents or mishaps and corrective actions.[31]

While the Office of Commercial Space Transportation is responsible for enforcing these informed consent requirements, it is prohibited by CSLAA from imposing any further safety requirements on launch companies flying commercial spaceflight participants.[32] In particular, it is restricted from imposing new regulations, such as issuing design requirements for seatbelts or escape hatches, which could affect the ability of commercial entities to innovate freely in areas of spacecraft design and development. This prohibition, which was originally set to expire in 2012, was extended to 2015 under the FAA Modernization and Reform Act of 2012[33] and then to October 2023 under the Commercial Space Launch Competitiveness Act of 2015.[34] According to 2016 testimony by the Government Accountability Office, experts believed that determining whether and when to regulate the safety of crew and spaceflight participants was one of FAA's most significant challenges.[35]

This Commercial Space Launch Competitiveness Act required FAA to submit an initial report to Congress in March 2018 and a follow-on report in 2022 on the commercial space industry's progress in developing voluntary safety standards for human spaceflight. These reports must be prepared in coordination with an industry advisory group and include observable metrics that would indicate readiness of the commercial space sector to transition to a more regulated safety regime without undermining the growth of the industry. The reports are also to include a framework for transitioning to a new regulatory regime.

FAA submitted its first report, "Evaluation of Commercial Human Space Flight Safety Frameworks and Key Indicators," to Congress in 2017. The report identified four types of metrics FAA proposes to use in determining whether greater federal regulation is appropriate:[36]

- Indicators of changes in the purpose of commercial space travel, such as moving beyond adventure travel to providing regular transportation to orbital space stations.
- Indicators of the size and complexity of the commercial spaceflight industry, such as the number of suppliers of orbital and suborbital commercial services and the existence of multiple suppliers of similar vehicles.

- Indicators of the industry's progress in developing voluntary safety standards, such as consensus safety standards and voluntary reporting.
- Indicators of FAA's readiness to provide expertise in human spaceflight safety and legal authorities to develop and implement a regulatory safety framework.

In February 2019, the Secretary of Transportation submitted a report to Congress recommending activities and regulatory action that would support establishment of a new safety framework and a proposed transition plan for the industry. The report found that, based on the readiness indicators, as of 2019, no commercial human spaceflight activities were ready to transition to a new safety framework that would involve regulatory action. This finding was based on the fact that, since the 2017 report identifying indicators of readiness, there had only been three FAA-licensed commercial launches carrying trained crew and no commercial launches with tourists aboard.[37]

Interagency Medical Standard Recommendations

Though federal law requires commercial spaceflight companies to inform passengers and crew of mission-related risks, certain medical conditions associated with spaceflight are still unknown or poorly understood. In 2012, FAA's Center of Excellence for Commercial Space Transportation issued a recommended set of comprehensive guidelines for medically screening crew and spaceflight participants ahead of tourist flights. The "Flight Crew Medical Standards and Spaceflight Participant Medical Acceptance Guidelines for Commercial Space Flight" was an attempt by FAA, NASA, and medical experts to provide a consolidated guide to medical screening practices that could be employed voluntarily by commercial operators and FAA.[38] The guidelines include a consensus set of passenger acceptance recommendations that could also serve as advice to commercial operators developing their own medical programs.

Recommended guidelines for suborbital flights included requiring commercial spaceflight participants to fill out a comprehensive medical questionnaire and undergo a physical examination by a physician with knowledge of the spaceflight environment. The guidelines recommended that the aerospace physician and vehicle operator develop, when possible, mitigation strategies and training regimens for any spaceflight participant who does not meet medical standards.

For orbital spaceflight, the guidelines recommend an additional mental health screening, as orbital spaceflight is associated with significant psychological stressors that underlying psychiatric or behavioral problems may exacerbate. Additionally, for orbital flights, the guidelines recommended chest X-rays, pregnancy tests, drug tests, pulmonary function testing, and exercise cardiovascular testing. Finally, the guidelines recommended post-flight medical evaluations and debriefings for spaceflight participants aboard orbital flights.[39]

[...]

Training Guidelines

Commercial crew and private astronaut pilots licensed by FAA to fly to space—or the edge of it—must meet certain training and medical standards, but those standards do not currently extend to spaceflight participants paying for a trip. Often, private astronauts that serve as pilots on space launch vehicles such as those flown by Virgin Galactic have significant NASA or military test pilot experience and thousands of flight hours. However, some private astronauts may need additional specialized training for certain missions such as docking with the ISS or using specific technologies. This year, NASA signed an agreement to partner with a private contracting firm to train such private astronauts at federal facilities[56] and provide aeromedical services prior to, during, and after private astronaut spaceflight missions.[57] While NASA works with private contractors on many mission support activities, this is the first NASA-sponsored contract for private astronaut training.

Insurance and Liability Issues

International governance regimes are in place to provide guidance about liability for space-related accidents. The United Nations Convention on International Liability Caused by Space Objects entered into force in 1972.[58] This agreement, which elaborates on Article VII of the Treaty on Principles Governing the Activities of States in the Exploration and Use of Outer Space, Including the Moon and Other Celestial Bodies (the Outer Space Treaty), stipulates that a state that launches an object to space shall be liable to pay compensation for damage caused by that object on the surface of Earth or to aircraft—but not for damage to a satellite in orbit.[59] According to the Outer Space Treaty, a nation is responsible for anything launched from its soil, including commercial spacecraft and payloads not owned or operated by the government. The treaty defines "damage" as loss of life, personal injury, or other impairment of health.[60]

Article VII of the Liability Convention would likely apply to an accident involving a vehicle launched from U.S. soil with foreign spaceflight participants aboard. However, the article stipulates that the provisions of the treaty do not apply to damage caused by a space object of a launching state to nationals of that state. In other words, compensation for injury to U.S. citizens and damage to property in the United States caused by a spacecraft launched from the United States would be entirely a matter of U.S. law and is not subject to the Outer Space Treaty.

In order to launch a rocket in the United States, a commercial launch operator must receive a license from FAA. One of the requirements for approval of a license is carriage of third-party liability insurance.[61] FAA requires an assessment of maximum probable financial loss (MPL) from any accident claim and proof that the operator either has financial reserves equal to the MPL estimate or has purchased that amount of liability insurance.

Federal law places a statutory cap of $500 million on third-party liability.[62] The original Space Launch Amendments Act, passed in 1988, makes the U.S. government responsible for covering damage beyond the $500 million cap.[63]

It is not clear whether that government coverage would extend to families of individuals aboard a commercial space vehicle that experiences an accident. Under informed consent agreements required by FAA, space tourists effectively waive the right to hold the launch operator liable for loss of life or injury. However, the families of spaceflight participants are not required to sign any such form and in theory could still sue the launch operator in the event of a catastrophic accident. Whether the informed consent waiver would preclude the award of damages in such a case has not been tested in court.[64]

Accident Investigation

There are no current federal guidelines delineating accident investigation jurisdiction should a commercial spaceflight accident occur with passengers on board. According to a nonbinding 2004 memorandum of understanding between FAA, the National Transportation Safety Board (NTSB), and the U.S. Air Force, the U.S. military will investigate any accident that occurs during a space launch aboard its rockets, and FAA and the NTSB will be responsible for investigating commercial accidents.[65]

FAA's Office of Space Transportation is responsible for overseeing investigations of all accidents associated with FAA-licensed space operations. However, by statute, the NTSB, an independent agency, could also have jurisdiction to investigate a commercial space accident when the board determines an accident related to the transportation of individuals is "catastrophic."[66] For example, the NTSB conducted the investigation into the crash of SpaceShipTwo, a Virgin Galactic-operated spacecraft that broke up in the air during a test flight, resulting in the death of the craft's copilot in 2014.[67] That spacecraft was insured under an aviation hull and liability policy by AIG for losses of $40 million to $50 million.[68] There has been debate in Congress since that time about whether the NTSB's authority over commercial spaceflight accident investigations needs to be more clearly codified in law and how jurisdiction should be shared between FAA and the NTSB.

Considerations for Congress

Congress most recently addressed subjects with implications for space tourism in the Commercial Space Launch Competitiveness Act of 2015. In that law, Congress determined that the nascent commercial space transportation industry should go through a "learning period" lasting until at least 2023 before it receives closer regulation by the federal government.[69] Given the development of the industry since that time, Congress may want to consider whether the law restricting FAA's authority to regulate the safety of commercial spacecraft with humans onboard should be extended, lifted, or allowed to expire in phases. Congress also has supported the development of voluntary safety standards by industry, interagency working groups, and the aerospace medical community, and may want to consider whether the federal government should adopt such standards as regulations.

The Department of Commerce's Office of Space Commerce has a regulatory role in commercial human spaceflight activities, pursuant to the department's statutory responsibility to "foster the conditions for the economic growth and technological advancement of the United States space commerce industry" (51 U.S.C. §50702(c)(1)). Likewise, the National Institute of Standards and Technology (NIST), a part of the department, has the authority to issue voluntary standards. To date, the department has not authored any such standards related to commercial space activities but has convened stakeholder workshops and issued best practice frameworks and standards in areas such as cybersecurity, genetic testing technologies, and other challenging technology sectors as roadmaps for industry development and self-governance.

The National Space Council operates as part of the Executive Office of the President to provide advice on civil, commercial, and military space issues and coordinate implementation of the President's space policies and strategies. The council is chaired by the Vice President and includes the Secretaries of State, Defense, Transportation, and Commerce, among other members.[70] In 2018, the council directed the Department of Commerce to generate a legislative proposal to establish an entity within the department for administering regulation of commercial spaceflight activities not overseen by FAA.[71] Such activities could potentially include asteroid mining, on-orbit satellite servicing, space traffic management, and other commercial endeavors. In 2018, the Department of Commerce proposed designating its Office of Commercial Space as an independent bureau with responsibility for commercial space traffic management, in addition to other functions. A bill to create such a bureau and assign it responsibility for regulating commercial spaceflight was introduced in the 115th Congress (H.R. 2809), but it did not advance.

The bill was reintroduced in the 116th Congress (H.R. 3610), with no further action to date. A September 2019 Senate Appropriations Committee report expressed concern that an independent space commerce bureau might not be equipped to fully replace the military's space traffic management role, and the committee recommended an independent review by the National Academy of Public Administration.[72]

Congress may at some point judge that the industry's progress is sufficient to justify a formal safety standard regime. In that circumstance, it could direct FAA to establish a licensing process for launch vehicles carrying human occupants.

Another option for congressional action would be hearings to examine expert or industry views on the need for closer government oversight of space tourism activities, to include launch and reentry as well as accommodations in orbit, if other than the ISS. Congress could also direct additional studies on some of these topics by organizations such as the National Academy of Public Administration, the National Academy of Sciences, or NIST.

Notes

1. CRS Report R45416, Commercial Space: Federal Regulation, Oversight, and Utilization, by Daniel Morgan.

2. Testimony of NASA Deputy Associate Administrator of Space Station Michael Hawes in U.S. Congress, House Committee on Science, Space, and Technology, Space Tourism, 107th Cong., 1st sess., June 26, 2001 (Washington, DC: GPO, 2001).

3. U.S. Congress, House Committee on Transportation and Infrastructure, Subcommittee on Aviation, Commercial Space Transportation, 111th Cong., 1st sess., December 2, 2009 (Washington, DC: GPO, 2009).

4. Northern Sky Research, "Space Tourism Market About to Take Off," December 17, 2019, at https://www.nsr.com/nsr-report-space-tourism-market-ready-to-take-off/.

25. Daniel Oberhaus, "How NASA Certifies New Spacecraft Safe Enough for Humans," Wired, May 13, 2020, at https://www.wired.com/story/how-nasa-certifies-new-spacecraft-safe-enough-for-humans.

26. 51 U.S.C. §50902(20).

27. Federal Aviation Administration,"Guidance on Informing Crew and Spaceflight Participants of Risk," FAA Office of Commercial Space Transportation, April 4, 2017, at https://www.faa.gov/space/licensing_process/regulations/media/Guidance_on_Informing_Crew_and_Space_Flight_Participants_of_Risk.pdf.

28. Federal Aviation Administration, "Human Space Flight Requirements for Crew and Space Flight Participants," 71 Federal Register 75615, December 15, 2006.

29. Ibid.

30. 14 C.F.R. §460.45.

31. Ibid.

32. P.L. 114-90, §111(5).

33 P.L. 112-95, §827.

34 P.L. 114-90§111(9).

35. U.S. Government Accountability Office, "Commercial Space: Industry Developments and FAA Challenges," Testimony before the Subcommittee on Aviation, Committee on Transportation and Infrastructure, House of Representatives, June 22, 2016.

36. Federal Aviation Administration, Report to Congress: FAA Evaluation of Commercial Human Space Flight Safety Frameworks and Key Industry Indicators, October 2017, at https://www.faa.gov/about/plans_reports/congress/media/ CSLCA_Sec111_Report_to_Congress.pdf.

37. Department of Transportation, "Report to Congress: U.S. Department of Transportation Evaluation of Commercial Human Space Flight Activities Most Appropriate for a New Safety Framework," February 26, 2019, at https://www.faa.gov/about/office_org/headquarters_offices/ast/advisory_committee/meeting_news/media/2019/may/ Section_111_Report_Summary_v3.pdf.

38. Federal Aviation Administration, Center of Excellence for Commercial Space Transportation, "Flight Crew Medical Standards and Spaceflight Participant Medical

Acceptance Guidelines for Commercial Space Flight," June 30, 2012, at http://coe-cst.org/flight-crew-medical-standards-and-spaceflight-participant-medical-acceptance-guidelines-for- commercial-space-flight.

39. Ibid.

56. Andrea Leinfelder, "Houston Company to Train Private Astronauts at NASA Facilities," Houston Chronicle, January 30, 2020, at https://www.houstonchronicle.com/business/bizfeed/article/Houston-company-to-train-private-astronauts-at-15016337.php.

57. KBR, "In a Space Industry First, NASA Grants KBR the Right to Train Private Astronauts at NASA Facilities," press release, January 30, 2020.

58. United Nations Office for Outer Space Affairs, "Convention on International Liability for Damage Caused by Space Objects," Committee on the Peaceful Uses of Outer Space, September 1972.

59. United Nations, "Treaty on Principles Governing the Activities of States in the Exploration and Use of Outer Space, Including the Moon and Other Celestial Bodies, Article VII," Committee on the Peaceful Uses of Outer Space, October 1967.

60. Carl Christol, "International Liability for Damage Caused by Space Objects," American Journal of International Law, vol. 74, no. 2, February 27, 2017, pp. 346-371.

61. 51 U.S.C. §50914.

62. Federal Aviation Administration, "Risk-Sharing Regime for U.S. Commercial Space Transportation," April 2002 at https://www.faa.gov/about/office_org/headquarters_offices/ast/media/FAALiabilityRiskSharing4-02.pdf.

63. Commercial Space Launch Act Amendments of 1988 (P.L. 100-657).

64. Jackie Wattles, "Why on Earth Would a Company Offer Insurance for Space Travel?" CNN Business, September 15, 2018, at https://money.cnn.com/2018/09/15/technology/business/space-insurance-industry/index.html.

65. Federal Aviation Administration, "Memorandum of Understanding Between the National Transportation Safety Board, Department of the Air Force, and Federal Aviation Administration Regarding Space Launch Accidents," September 2004, at https://www.faa.gov/about/office_org/headquarters_offices/ast/media/ mou_space_launch_accidents.pdf.

66. 49 U.S.C. §1131.

67. Alwyn Scott, "Spacesuit? Helmet? Life Insurance? Space Tourist Loophole May End," Reuters, November 5, 2014, at https://www.reuters.com/article/us-space-crash-virgin-insurance-analysis/spacesuit-helmet-life-insurance-space- tourist-loophole-may-end-idUSKBN0IP2XO20141106.

68. Carolyn Cohn and Richa Naidu, "Virgin Galactic Spaceship Insured for $40-$50 Million, Lead Underwriter, AIG: Sources," Reuters, November 3, 2014, at https://www.reuters.com/article/us-space-crash-virgin-insurance/virgin-galactic-spaceship-insured-for-40-50-million-lead-underwriter-aig-sources-idUSKBN0IN0SP20141103.

69. P.L. 114-90, §111(5).

70. Executive Order 13803, "Reviving the National Space Council," 82 Federal Register 31429, July 7, 2017.

71. White House, Office of the Press Secretary, "Space Policy Directive–2, Streamlining Regulations on Commercial Use of Space," presidential memorandum, May 24, 2018, at https://www.whitehouse.gov/presidential-actions/space-policy-directive-2-streamlining-regulations-commercial-use-space/.

72. S. Rept. 116-127.

A Sufficient Level of Safety Has Not Yet Been Established for Suborbital Spaceflight

Sam Dinkin

Sam Dinkin is a regular contributor and columnist for the Space Review, *an online publication that provides articles and commentary on many aspects of space exploration. He is based in Austin, Texas.*

With the 737 MAX in the news for being risky, it is timely to remember that airline travel in general is astonishingly safe. As of 2018, the overall risk of death was one fatal accident per three million flights. It will take many decades, at the earliest, for suborbital travel to reach this safety milestone. Regular Mars service may be able to match the safety rate per kilometer traveled (one death per 80 billion passenger-kilometers) with less than 1,500 non-fatal trips in a row given the minimum Earth-Mars distance of 54.6 million kilometers.

If the risk of death per suborbital trip is high, it is unlikely that businesses will permit key individuals to travel via point-to-point suborbital spaceflight. One possible standard for the risk being low is to compare the risk of point-to-point suborbital spaceflight to other risky, but legal, forms of transportation. An 800-kilometer trip by motorcycle takes about as long to complete, door-to-door, as a trip via airplane. At 109 deaths per billion kilometers, there is a 1 in 11,500 chance of dying on an 800-kilometer motorcycle trip, which means a decrease in life expectancy of one day per 31.5 years of life expectancy. That is about the same as the life expectancy of an executive who is 52 years old. The average age of a "C-suite" executive (CEO, CFO, CIO, etc.) is 54 years old.

Depending on how productive an executive is while in transit, a company might be willing to let an executive trade a

"How Safe Is Safe Enough for Point-to-Point Suborbital?" by Sam Dinkin, *The Space Review*, April 22, 2019. Reprinted by permission.

day of life expectancy for an extra day not in transit. If point-to-point suborbital travel can meet this 1-in-11,500 trip standard and the transit time is reduced by 24 hours, that might be safe enough. (And motorcycle travel might be unsafe enough to have travel policy not reimburse mileage for business motorcycle trips.)

If there are 11,500 suborbital point-to-point representative spaceflights, in a row, that are successful, that might retire enough risk for businesses to consider approving this form of transportation. Representative flights would need to be of sufficient reentry velocity to reflect the likely reentry velocity in a long-distance suborbital flight. Almost all of the risk is likely to be during launch and reentry, so sufficiently high reentry velocity flights that merely go up and down may suffice as being representative.

The best representative flight would be to match a potential suborbital travel route. Regular suborbital package delivery at human-survivable acceleration and deceleration levels might defray the cost of risk retirement.

An orbital launch and reentry is likely riskier than a suborbital launch and reentry. A total of 11,500 successful orbital flights in a row with no fatalities might also demonstrate that a rocket is safe enough for point-to-point suborbital travel. Travelers to orbit, the Moon, and Mars are likely to accept Soyuz and Space Shuttle levels of risk—approximately one fatal accident per 81 launches—at least at first. Retiring risk via orbital trips could permit commercial orbital service to enable continued improvement in safety levels until suborbital point-to-point travel is demonstrated to be safe enough.

Even at prices of $1 million per orbital launch, versus $62 million today, 11,500 launches would cost $11.5 billion, and would take 31.5 years at the rate of one launch per day. This is likely the most obvious obstacle demonstrating why suborbital point-to-point passenger travel will be unlikely to be a $20 billion per year industry by 2030 (see "Could suborbital point-to-point really be worth $20 billion a year in 2030?" *The Space Review*, March 25, 2019). There are other reasons that are less obvious but may still delay the offering of suborbital point-to-point passenger service even longer than proving this level of safety.

CHAPTER 2

Should Space Militarization Be Accepted by the International Community?

Overview: Space Militarization Has a Long History

Dave Webb

Dave Webb is an emeritus professor of peace and conflict studies at Leeds Beckett University in the United Kingdom. His research interests include mobile technology and disaster relief. He also served as a fellow of the Royal Astronomical Society.

Scientific, military and civilian activities in space have always been controversial, involving questions such as:

- Can scientific missions in space be separated from military activities?
- Are scientific missions in space a way of justifying and improving military activities?
- Do the military developments in space make the world safer or more dangerous?
- How do we justify so much money being spent on this type of high technology when there are so many other issues (such as climate change, pandemics, social programs, etc.) that need to be financed?
- What are the short- and long-term environmental consequences of this activity?

In a democratic society it is often argued that, for a particular project to obtain funds from the public purse, it has to be approved and scrutinized by a democratically elected government or its appointed servants. So, individuals do not need to justify their participation in these projects as they have already been sanctioned by society. However, others argue that people should make their own moral and ethical judgements especially when public policies

Taken from "The Nuclearisation and Militarisation of Space—A Brief History," by Dave Webb, The Global Network, 2000, revised 2021. Reprinted by permission.

may have been arrived at through compromise, misinformation and/or powerful lobbying by vested interests.

Space Use

Space rockets are often thought of in terms of space exploration and discovery. However, space users are predominantly commercial and a major player in the development of space technologies is the military.

In recent years there has been an increased dependency on the use of space technology. Satellite navigation systems are being used for vehicle and pedestrian journeys, to track goods and vehicles. Satellite systems are also employed for communications and entertainment, international financial transactions, air-traffic management and weather, environment and climate monitoring.

In 2020 there was a total of 114 launches from 21 launch sites, with 10 failures.[1] Also in 2021, 1,283 satellites were placed in orbit, the highest number of satellites launched in a year so far[2]—although even more are set to be launched in 2021. At the end of April 2021 there was a total of 7,389 satellites in space, of which only around 3,368 are still active.[3] The majority of launches are currently from private industry and developments in mini-satellite technologies, the rapidly increasing number of launch sites and lower cost of launches has also resulted in constellations of tens of thousands of communications satellites being established in orbits relatively close to the Earth to give constant super-fast global coverage.

Space is now big business and with some forecasters suggesting it could be worth over $1 trillion by 2040.[4] In 2020 global government spending on space totalled $82.5 billion.[5] The United States topped the spending at $47.7 billion (58% of the world total) with China as second highest at $8.9 billion followed by France, Russia and Japan. The total global annual expenditure for military space systems is also rising and exceeded $28 billion in 2020.

A growing number of countries have now built satellites, but as of 2019, eleven countries have had the capability to send objects into orbit using their own launch vehicles. Russia and Ukraine inherited the space launchers and satellites capability from the Soviet Union, following its dissolution in 1991.

The increase in space militarization has seen a number of space-focused defence organizations being established in the last five years, including the Russian Space Forces (2015), China's PLA Strategic Support Force (2015), the U.S. Space Force (2019), India's Defence Space Agency (2019), the French Space Command (2019), Japan's Space Operation Squadron (2020), NATO Space Centre (2020) and the UK Space Command (2021).

Billionaires and their corporations are also developing plans for space tourism, space transport and the mining of asteroids and planets. However, the launching of rockets is also producing environmental problems, polluting the ground with fuel and exhaust fumes. The passage of rockets through the atmosphere could also be affecting the ozone layer[6] and depositing black carbon and alumina particles in the stratosphere with possible effects on the weather and climate.[7]

The increased activity in space is also creating large amounts of space junk. The European Space Agency has estimated that there are roughly 166 million man-made objects in space, ranging in size from one millimetre to the size of a refrigerator.[8] As launch numbers rise and as tens of thousands of satellites with a limited life-time are placed in orbit, the problem will increase significantly. In 1978 NASA scientist Donald J. Kessler proposed a situation where two colliding objects in space could generate more debris that then collides with other objects, creating even more. This has become known as the Kessler Syndrome,[9] and such a self-sustaining cascade of collisions could result in a cloud of debris travelling at 36,000 km/hr that becomes so dense that rockets may not be able to penetrate it.

The major players in the development of space systems have, in the past, been the United States and the Soviet Union (and now Russia)—but more recently Europe (through the European Space Agency, ESA), China, India and France have become important players and around 72 countries now have space programmes, including Brazil, Japan, Canada, South Korea and the UAE. The UK is also becoming active and now has the highest number of private space start-ups after the U.S.

In the Beginning

Before the commercialisation of space, the first scientific and explorative space missions employed hardware that had been originally developed for military purposes and the race to send astronauts to the moon was politically motivated.

The initial development of modern-day space technologies began in 1930s Germany with the work of Nazi rocket pioneers led by Wernher von Braun. Their V2 missiles were constructed at Mittelwerk in tunnels under Kohnstein Mountain by slave labour from concentration camps. Around one half of the 60,000 prisoners used to build the rockets died of starvation and abuse and more people were killed in the construction of the rockets than the rockets killed at their targets.[10]

At the end of the war von Braun and his team were taken to the U.S. by the U.S. Army in a programme known as "Operation Paperclip"[11] and von Braun's group produced the first Inter Continental Ballistic Missiles (ICBMs) and the Saturn V, which was used by the U.S. to launch their astronauts into space.

The Soviet Union also took their share of German scientists from von Braun's team and the V-2 technology was copied for their first missile, the R-1, a later version of which (the R-7) was used to launch Sputnik 1, the world's first artificial satellite, in 1957.

However, it was Arthur C. Clarke in 1945 who first suggested using satellites for global communications. He thought though, that many would consider this idea "too far-fetched to be taken seriously." The RAND Corporation first proposed a military satellite system in 1946. The weight of an atomic bomb payload at that time meant that there was little prospect of them being carried by rockets for many years. In fact, the U.S. started its ICBM programmes in 1954—after the development of the smaller and more powerful hydrogen bomb (first tested on 1st November 1952) required smaller, less accurate rockets.

On 28th July 1955 the U.S. announced its intention to launch a satellite to study the upper atmosphere during the International Geophysical Year (IGY—a worldwide scientific event from 15th July 1957 to 31st December 1958). It was intended that this programme would follow National Security Council (NSC) recommendations (laid out in May 1955) to effectively separate the military and civilian sectors of the U.S. space effort. The Soviets also announced the intention to launch a satellite, which they duly did.

The Space Race

The Soviet Union had detonated their first hydrogen bomb in August 1952 and this, together with the launch of Sputnik 1, a small 58 cm (23 in) diameter polished metal sphere, launched into a low elliptical Earth in 1957, caused general panic in the United States. The Soviet Union now had the capability to reach (and possibly target) anywhere on the planet from their own territory. Therefore, this event launched not only a space race but also a new type of arms race and space technology developed in the U.S. and the U.S.S.R. through the political and military competitiveness of the Cold War. At the end of the Cold War, U.S. and U.S.S.R. military space systems were providing key functions for command, control, communications, computer, intelligence, surveillance and reconnaissance (C4ISR) in addition to important early warning, navigation and weapons guidance applications.

In July 1958 the U.S. government passed The National Aeronautics and Space Act, which officially divided the civilian and military sectors and created the National Aeronautics and Space Administration (NASA). NASA opened on 1st October 1958 and was the brainchild of James R. Killian, scientific advisor to President Eisenhower. Killian and Eisenhower devised NASA to be a strictly civilian enterprise, thereby limiting the military's role in the national space program. However, Congress wanted a much stronger military role in space and so created the Civilian-

Military Liaison Committee (to coordinate NASA and Department of Defense [DOD] activities) and the National Aeronautics and Space Council (chaired by the president as commander in chief of the U.S. military to create national space policy). NASA's first major project was the Mercury programme to send a man into low-Earth orbit. At the same time long-term planning for Apollo, the U.S. Moon program, began.

The importance of space support for navigation and communications was recognized early in the space era. The U.S. Navy launched the world's first military navigational satellite system, Transit lA, in September 1959 and used it to improve the accuracy of Polaris submarines to about 1 mile. The U.S. Army launched the first military communication satellite, Courier lB, on 4 October 1960.

The first U.S. Antiballistic Missile (ABM) test launch took place on 16th December 1959. However, the programme was cancelled in May 1959 because the mechanical tracking radars were too slow, and the computers were not powerful enough. However, in the 1960s the Soviet Union and the U.S. developed anti-satellite (ASAT) systems that used systems developed for defence against ballistic missiles armed with nuclear warheads. At that time the accuracy of the interceptor guidance systems was limited but the large range of the nuclear warheads would enable the success of an ASAT or ABM strike.

The North American Air Defense Command (NORAD) became operational on 12th September 1957 to detect and report on any ICBM attack on the North American continent. In October 1960, NORAD took on space defence with the formation of the space detection and tracking system. NORAD's missions were:

1. warning of ballistic missile attack,
2. defense against manned bomber attack, and
3. space surveillance.

An important component of the missile warning system was, and still is, the Ballistic Missile Early Warning System (BMEWS) which includes powerful radar systems in Alaska, at Thule in Greenland and at Fylingdales in North Yorkshire.

[…]

NASA—The Military Options

After the end of the Apollo programme the funding for NASA fell sharply. It became U.S. government policy that NASA become more involved in co-operative ventures with commercial and military projects.

In the 80s NASA and U.S. Space Command joined forces to release spy satellites during classified shuttle missions and agreed to work together in: "several areas of mutual interest in the hopes of saving both organisations costs and sharing in new technologies to benefit future spaceflight and spacecraft." Partnership teams were formed to study:

- the launching of Defense Support Program satellites from the Space Shuttle in 1999;
- the use of the Shuttle for Air Force technology payloads;
- space transportation needs of NASA and the U.S. Air Force;
- respective infrastructures and common-use facilities;
- the problem of orbiting space debris; and
- expanded cooperation in space weather environment research and data sharing.

In addition, NASA and the Ballistic Missile Defense Organization (BMDO) jointly sponsored The Deep Space Program Science Experiment (DSPSE), launched in early 1994. In 1997, the Air Force Research Laboratory and NASA created the Space Technology Alliance to coordinate the development of affordable, effective space technologies. The DOD also gave $200 million to NASA to help pay for the space shuttle *Endeavour*'s January 2000 mission to create high resolution, three-dimensional maps of the Earth.

Militarisation of Space

Satellites are now commonly used by the military for global positioning and navigation, early warning, missile targeting & guidance, communications, and surveillance, and the information they provide is used by military commanders to monitor battlefields, develop their strategy, organise their forces and target their weapons. The increasing importance of satellites in the surveillance and management of modern warfare has led to the recognition that, in order to retain control and ensure communications, important military satellites need to be protected. This is a major reason for the increase in research into weapons systems to defend spacecraft and even threaten "enemy" space-based systems.

The U.S. Space Command's "Vision 2020," published in 1997,[12] argued that the protection of space requires superior U.S. space warfare capability and proclaims itself "stewards for military space" and sets out two principle themes:

1. dominating the space dimension of military operations to protect U.S. interests and investment
2. integrating space forces into warfighting capabilities across the full spectrum of conflict

It also recognised and accepted the growing division between the global economic "haves" and "have-nots" and introduced the doctrine of "full spectrum dominance" (the military domination of the land, sea, air, space and information) to protect the interests of the "haves."

This "vision" was to be achieved by a "Long Range Plan," the "Guiding Principles" of which are:

- Space is an enabler of military operations. Space-based sensors provide information on which forces depend and virtually all other information flows through space;
- Commercial space explosion—industry growing at 20% pa, 1000+ satellites to be launched and $500 billion spent worldwide over the next few years;

- Space is an emerging area of vital national interest, critical to military and economic instruments of power;
- We will be challenged;
- Military must be ready—the nation's growing dependence on space cannot become a vulnerability—having the ability to deny an enemy's use of space will grow in importance.

The adopted methodology involved four operational concepts:

- Control of Space: assure freedom to operate, deny the enemy;
- Global Engagement: which includes worldwide situational awareness, defence against ballistic and cruise missiles and the capability to hold at risk from space a small number of high value targets. Provision of a dominant battlespace awareness enabling on-demand targeting and engagement of all ballistic and cruise missiles;
- Full Force Integration: warfighters to take full advantage of space capabilities as an integral part of special, joint and combined warfare;
- Global Partnerships: strengthening military space capabilities through the leveraging of civil, commercial, intelligence, national and international space efforts.

At the time General Joseph Ashy (ex Commander in Chief U.S. Space Command) said: *"It's politically sensitive, but it's going to happen ... Some people don't want to hear this, and it sure isn't in vogue, but—absolutely—we're going to fight in space. We're going to fight from space and we're going to fight into space ... That's why the U.S. has development programs in directed energy and hit-to-kill mechanisms."*[13]

A U.S. Air Force board report also stated that: *"In the next two decades, new technologies will allow the fielding of space-based weapons of devastating effectiveness to be used to deliver energy and mass as force projection in tactical and strategic conflict.... These advances will enable lasers ... to effect very many kills."*[14]

These plans were (and remain) worrying to other national leaders and governments. Speaking in Geneva in January 1999, UN

Secretary General Kofi Annan urged the UN's annual Conference on Disarmament to *"codify principles which can ensure that outer space remains weapons-free."*

At the end of 2019, when Donald Trump authorised the U.S. Space Force, he said that it marked "*a big moment*" and that there was "*going to be a lot of things happening in space. Because space is the world's newest warfighting domain.*"[15] U.S. Secretary of Defense Mark Esper was quoted as saying that "*outer space has evolved into a warfighting domain ... Maintaining American dominance in that domain is now the mission of the United States Space Force.*"

Other nations are also joining the new space race and, although Russia, China and India have had extensive military space programs for some time, others like Japan, South Korea and NATO are joining in. France has also allocated 3.6 billion euros to its own military space force and in 2019 the U.K. defense secretary announced a £30 million military space programme for the development of small satellites. Mordaunt announced that: "*Today we show the sky is no longer the limit for our Armed Forces,*" and also talked of being "*the first partner in Operation Olympic Defender,*" a U.S.-led international coalition aimed at deterring "*hostile actions by rivals.*"

[...]

Notes

1. "Spaceflight in 2020" from Wikipedia—https://en.wikipedia.org/wiki/2020_in_spaceflight
2. "Outer Space Objects Index," United Nations Office for Outer Space Affairs. https://www.unoosa.org/oosa/osoindex/index.jspx?lf_id=
3. "How Many Satellites Are Orbiting the Earth in 2021?" by Nibedita Mohanta, Geospatial World—https://www.geospatialworld.net/blogs/how-many-satellites-are-orbiting-the-earth-in-2021/
4. "Space: Investing in the Final Frontier," Morgan Stanley. https://www.morganstanley.com/Themes/global-space-economy
5. "Government Space Budgets Surge Despite Global Pandemic" by Simon Seminari. http://interactive.satellitetoday.com/via/march-2021/government-space-budgets-surge-despite-global-pandemic/
6. "Rocket Launches May Need Regulation to Prevent Ozone Depletion, Says Study," Science Daily, 1 April 2009—https://www.sciencedaily.com/releases/2009/03/090331153014.htm

7. "How Much Pollution Is Produced by Rockets?" by Leonard Davy, Scientific American. https://www.scientificamerican.com/article/how-much-air-pollution-is-produced-by-rockets/

8. "Space Debris by Numbers," European Space Agency. https://www.esa.int/Safety_Security/Space_Debris/Space_debris_by_the_numbers

9. "Kessler Syndrome," Wikipedia—https://en.wikipedia.org/wiki/Kessler_syndrome

10. "Sabotaging the German V-2 Rocket," by Lori Samlin Miller, June 15, 2019. https://www.aish.com/ho/p/Sabotaging-the-German-V-2-Rocket.html

11. "What Was Operation Paperclip?" by Thomas D. McAvoy, History. com. https://www.history.com/news/what-was-operation-paperclip

12. "Vision 2020" by U.S. Space Command, from The Community, https://thecommunity.com/vision-2020-the-us-space-command/

13. Commander-in-Chief of U.S. Space Command, Joseph W. Ashy, Aviation Week and Space Technology, August 9, 1996, quoted from Master of Space by Karl Grossman, Progressive Magazine, January 2000

14. U.S. Air Force Advisory Board, "New World Vistas: Air and Space Power for the 21st Century," Space Technology Volume, 1996

15. "Trump Officially Establishes U.S. Space Force with 2020 Defense Bill Signing," by Leonard David, December 21, 2019. https://www.space.com/trump-creates-space-force-2020-defense-bill.html

Space Militarization Is a Necessary Aspect of National Security

Frank A. Rose

Frank A. Rose was a senior fellow and the co-director of the Center for Security, Strategy, and Technology in the Foreign Policy program at the Brookings Institution. He is currently serving as the principal deputy administrator for national nuclear security at the Department of Energy.

At the North Atlantic Treaty Organization's (NATO) December 2019 Leader's Summit in London, leaders acknowledged that technology is rapidly changing the international security environment, stating: "To stay secure, we must look to the future together. We are addressing the breadth and scale of new technologies to maintain our technological edge." Leaders also identified outer space as a key area of focus. They declared that "space [is] an operational domain for NATO, recognizing its importance in keeping us safe and tackling security challenges, while upholding international law." NATO defense ministers had previously approved an initial space policy in June 2019, but the details of that policy have not been publicly released.

Given the increasing role outer space is playing in NATO military operations, and the growing anti-satellite threat from states like Russia and China, NATO's decision to declare outer space an operational domain was the correct one. The key question now is: How can the alliance develop an effective implementation strategy to ensure it can maintain assured access to outer space and space-derived data?

Such a strategy will require several elements. First, NATO will need to improve its understanding of the anti-satellite threat. Second, outer space will need to be "mainstreamed" within NATO,

"NATO and Outer Space: Now What?" by Frank A. Rose, The Brookings Institution, April 22, 2020. Reprinted by permission.

especially with regard to the defense planning and operations process. Third, NATO will need to improve cooperation and coordination with the United States, the alliance's leader on outer space issues. Fourth, NATO should identify areas where it might work with the European Union (EU) on outer space. And finally, the alliance will need to find a way incorporate diplomacy into any eventual strategy.

The Emerging Anti-Satellite Threat

The threat to U.S. and allied space systems from anti-satellite weapons continues to grow. As former Director of National Intelligence Dan Coats noted in testimony before Congress in January 2019: "China and Russia are training and equipping their military space forces and fielding new anti-satellite weapons to hold U.S. and allied space systems at risk." Coats' testimony is complemented by numerous reports and studies by government and non-governmental organizations like the Defense Intelligence Agency, the National Air and Space Intelligence Center, the Center for Strategic and International Studies, and the Secure World Foundation.

NATO has also been the victim of real-world anti-satellite activities. In March 2019, the Norwegian government accused Russia of "harassing" communications systems during NATO exercises. Recent press reporting notes that the Norwegian Intelligence Service has documented a number of incidents in which "GPS signals and other secured communications between the Norwegian Armed forces, or NAF, units engaged in exercises were subjected to 'blocking' measures from sites located in Russia." And just last week, U.S. Space Command released a statement claiming that on April 15th, Russia had conducted a direct-ascent anti-satellite missile test. Faced with these real threats, how should NATO respond?

Improve Intelligence-Sharing

Collective action by NATO on outer space security issues will only happen when allies reach a consensus on the anti-satellite threat. As a first step, an appropriate organization at NATO (e.g., the Assistant Secretary General for Intelligence) should be directed to develop a comprehensive assessment of the anti-satellite threat to the alliance.

To be successful, this effort will require the full support of the U.S. intelligence community. Additionally, NATO officials should ensure relevant alliance political and military bodies (e.g., the North Atlantic Council, Military Committee, Senior Political Committee, and Defense Policy and Planning Committee) receive regular updates on the anti-satellite threat.

Mainstream Outer Space at NATO

NATO should ensure that outer space is "mainstreamed" and fully integrated within alliance political and military institutions, and is not treated as merely a "novelty item." For instance, overall responsibility for outer space should be placed in an organization like the Office of the Assistant Secretary General for Defense Policy and Planning, or the Office of the Assistant Secretary General for Defense Investment, which are responsible for defense policy, planning, and capability investment at NATO. Furthermore, noting the interrelationship between outer space and other domains like nuclear and cyber, NATO will need to establish mechanisms that encourage effective coordination and cooperation across the entire organization, including the military commands.

At the operational level, the alliance should ensure that outer space is incorporated in its major military exercises and wargames. This is critical because if NATO ever comes into a major conflict with Russia, one of Russia's first targets would be the alliance's space assets and space-derived information. Therefore, it is important for NATO to conduct its exercises with this in mind. Allied Command Transformation, NATO's warfare development command, should be tasked to make this a reality.

Ensure Cooperation and Coordination with the United States

At the end of the day, NATO's ultimate effectiveness in outer space will depend on its cooperation with the alliance's most important space power: the United States. To date, U.S. leadership has been the key driver of NATO decision making on outer space, and senior U.S. officials have actively engaged the alliance leadership. For example, in October 2019, General John Raymond, commander of U.S. Space Command and chief of space operations, briefed the NATO Military Committee on outer space security issues. These types of senior-level engagements between U.S. political and military leaders should continue and be expanded.

In addition to senior-level engagements, there are a number of other actions NATO and the United States could take to improve cooperation and coordination. Specifically, they should establish clear consultative mechanisms between NATO, U.S. Space Command, and the U.S. Space Force. One relatively easy step that could be taken quickly would be to establish a NATO liaison officer at U.S. Space Command and/or U.S. Space Force headquarters. Indeed, a number of allied officers are currently attached as liaisons at several U.S. combatant commands like U.S. Strategic Command (STRATCOM).

The United States should also seek to incorporate NATO representatives into its outer space-related wargames where possible, especially the Schriever Wargame, the premier U.S. space wargame. According to a U.S. Air Force press release, several allies including Australia, Canada, New Zealand, the United Kingdom, France, Germany, and Japan, have participated in previous Schriever Wargames. The United States should invite NATO political and military officials to participate in the next Schriever Wargame.

Cooperate with the EU

NATO should also explore ways to cooperate with the EU on outer space, primarily because the EU has developed and deployed the Galileoglobal navigation satellite system, which like the U.S.

Global Position System (GPS), provides accurate positioning and timing information. In particular, Galileo includes a capability known as the Public Regulated Service (PRS), an encrypted navigation service for governmental authorized users and sensitive applications that require high continuity. In a crisis situation, PRS could provide NATO important redundancy against an adversary's attempt to jam or destroy GPS. While many members of NATO are also members of the EU and have access to PRS, non-EU NATO members, and NATO as an organization, currently does not. Therefore, NATO should begin consultations with the EU about the possibility of gaining access to PRS for the alliance.

Don't Forget Diplomacy

Military solutions alone will not allow the United States and its allies to address the increasing anti-satellite threat. While I have generally supported many of the Trump administration's space security initiatives like the re-establishment of U.S. Space Command, a key element missing from the Trump administration's outer space security strategy has been the complete lack of a diplomatic component. Without a more comprehensive strategy that includes a strong diplomatic element, it will make it difficult for NATO to maintain enough political cohesion to pursue effective military policies. These tensions were highlighted in a recent article that noted: "With the exception of France and the United Kingdom, many Europeans countries are deeply uncomfortable with, or down right opposed to, the development and use of weapons in space."

This is not a problem unique to outer space. Throughout its history, there has been constant tension within NATO over the appropriate balance between defense and diplomacy in its strategy. Since the late 1960s, with the approval of the Harmel Report, named after former Belgian foreign minister Pierre Harmel, NATO has sought to more effectively balance some of the inherent tensions between defense and diplomacy. One of the key findings from the Harmel Report was that "military security and a policy of détente are not contradictory but complementary." Arms control was considered an essential element of this strategy. The general Harmel Report approach has shaped the key strategic decisions that the alliance has taken over the past 50 years, most notably the "Double-Track" decision in 1979 to deploy intermediate-range nuclear forces in Western Europe, while simultaneously engaging the Soviet Union in arms control negotiations.

As part of its overall strategy for outer space, NATO should develop options and recommendations on how it can advance diplomatic solutions to address the emerging threat to outer space systems. In particular, NATO should task the Arms Control and Disarmament Committee to examine what role the alliance could play in developing norms of behavior to encourage responsible use of outer space. And even though the Trump administration has generally been opposed to arms control, it has expressed openness to the development of norms for outer space. In an recent speech, Assistant Secretary of State Christopher Ford stated: "We clearly need to do more to develop non-legally–binding international norms of responsible behavior that are complementary to the existing legal regime."

U.S. Leadership Will Be Key

With the increasing role that outer space is playing in military operations, and the rise of the anti-satellite threat, NATO was correct in its decision to declare space as an operational domain in December 2019. The question now is whether the alliance will be able to translate this broad political guidance into an effective strategy.

An effective NATO strategy for outer space will depend on the ability of the alliance to build consensus on the threat; mainstream outer space into NATO's political and military institutions; find ways to cooperate with the EU; and incorporate diplomacy into that strategy. But at the end of the day, all of this will require clear, sustained, and consistent U.S. leadership.

The Creation of the US Space Force Plays an Essential Role in Protecting US Assets and Asserting US Leadership

Mir Sadat and Michael Sinclair

Mir Sadat is a former National Security Council policy director and founding editor-in-chief of the Space Force Journal. *Michael Sinclair is an active-duty Coast Guard captain and former deputy legal adviser at the National Security Council who is now a federal executive fellow at the Brookings Institution.*

Defense Secretary Lloyd Austin faces a host of challenges that are rapidly outpacing fiscal calendars, election cycles and even the best laid military plans based on last century's industrial age.

Nowhere is that more true than in space, which is vital to U.S. national security, commerce and the comfort of our modern life.

But while the military now treats space as a warfighting domain, it is still not poised to seize and hold the high ground for years to come.

The new secretary of defense has five urgent tasks to disrupt the status quo thinking in the Pentagon:

First, the Pentagon chief must challenge U.S. Space Command and the U.S. Space Force to provide a clear, bipartisan path forward toward mission execution that in the short, medium and eventually long-term emphasizes space as critical infrastructure that can be funded and grown beyond fiscal years and over successive presidential administrations.

Today, the military is focused on "look down" operations and the defense of United States space assets that facilitate those operations. Make no mistake, this is a critically important defense mission: both our way of warfighting and our modern way of life rely heavily on space-based services as critical infrastructure in

"A Pentagon Strategy for Elevating the Space Mission," by Mir Sadat and Michael Sinclair, Politico LLC, February 11, 2021. Reprinted by permission.

and of itself and as a key component for other types of critical infrastructure. China and Russia are well aware of space as critical infrastructure and are developing their own space defense and denial capabilities to level the playing field against traditionally overwhelming American commercial and military might. These challenges require the development of resilient space systems supporting worldwide voice communications; internet access; precision navigation and timing; security surveillance; terrestrial, air and maritime domain awareness; climate research; non-proliferation monitoring; and intelligence collection. Concentrating expertise to address these challenges is the reason why Space Force and Space Command came (back) into existence.

Throughout the 2020s, space activity—especially commercial space activity—will accelerate as new actors, both national and commercial, get in the game. More satellites and spacecraft mean greater urgency to mitigate risks associated with space debris proliferation, traffic management, protected orbits and access to space resources.

Protecting commercial, scientific and military objects in space requires surveillance and defense services in and throughout the domain of space, beyond just the "look down" capabilities that constrain today's space defense thinking. As such, Pentagon space operations need the long-range vision, capabilities, human talent, and authorities for the next phase of space operations in the medium-term, and they should pursue these things now, primarily through effective Congressional engagement and visionary multi-year budget builds.

Space systems are often notoriously slow to develop, myopically designed and expensive to deploy, maintain and upgrade. Space defense readiness authorities and appropriations must anticipate the foreseeable trend of greater numbers of space actors (including a likely growth in human space flight), acting farther out from Earth, while the United States still has the opportunity to lead in the domain. Failing to do so may have a transformational, if not existential, impact on the United States' ability to successfully meet security and global competitiveness challenges over the next century.

Second, Austin must emphasize investments like those identified in the military's 2060 North-Star Space Vision published in 2019 that encourages an integrated approach that contemplates U.S. government coordination and consultation with private industry, scientific communities and academia. In short, the Department of Defense must look for opportunities to prioritize investment in exponential technologies that will allow the United States to qualitatively leap-frog over our rivals and ensure that we exit the current era of strategic competition on top.

Third, Austin should fully exercise his role as co-equal partner (albeit with a big budget) with the other cabinet secretaries to champion creating "whole of government" solutions to space challenges. While there are a great many space activities in this fast approaching future state that demand defense leadership, there are many that do not. Space traffic management, space debris removal, planetary protection (as distinguished from planetary defense), climate research, on-orbit satellite servicing and eventually space search and rescue need not necessarily be the mission responsibility of Space Command. Planetary defense though likely should be.

Thus, the defense secretary must work across the federal government with space responsibilities such as NASA and the Departments of State, Commerce, Transportation, and Homeland Security to nail down who is going to be responsible for what. There is existing Executive-level guidance to help facilitate this.

Fourth, The Space Force will no doubt help the United States confront serious challenges and threats in, to and from space, and it will also exercise "out-of-the-box" thinking to capitalize on the great opportunities space provides for the nation. Immediately, and for its own credibility, the secretary of defense must direct the Space Force to create a timeline and showcase its own projects and ways of doing business that defy the delays and procurement missteps that have plagued so many past defense activities.

Fifth, the new secretary of defense should commend President Biden for providing a statement of support and affirmation to thousands of uniformed and civilian personnel of the Space Force. The new administration's clear stance on retaining the new branch finally puts an end to conspiratorial rumors and goes a long way toward safeguarding the morale of the Guardians who have experienced the inevitable uncertainty, organizational turbulence and legacy frictions inherent in standing up the first new armed force in over 70 years.

The raw potential of space provides a once-in-a-generation opportunity to capitalize on the nation's growing space enthusiasm to ensure better access to and diversify careers in science, technology, engineering and mathematics; promote research and development and economic growth in technologically under-served areas; and to help bring renewed focus on space solutions for vital climate research, tracking endangered species and detecting the mass migration of humans due to weather, war or otherwise.

Fully realizing this potential can continue a legacy of American bipartisan space leadership that traces its lineage back to the Kennedy administration. It can help chart a better path for space security and governance that advances democratic norms and values; ethical business practices; human rights; environmental and social conscientiousness; and financial transparency. But our example and leadership must be so profound that other nations will have no choice but to follow and replicate our success here on Earth and in space.

Not Enough Is Being Done to Prevent the Weaponization of Space

Nayef Al-Rodhan

Nayef Al-Rodhan is an honorary fellow at St. Antony's College, University of Oxford, and a senior fellow and head of the Geopolitics and Global Futures Programme at the Geneva Centre for Security Policy.

Space weaponization is not a new phenomenon. However, a large number of technological developments over the past few decades have led to a drastic acceleration in the destructive potential of space warfare. In 2016, the Russian Deputy Foreign Minister Sergey Ryabkov voiced his concerns about the possibility of weapons being deployed in space. His statement followed advancements in technological endeavours such as the Prompt Global Strike program, a project within which the United States started developing hypersonic glide vehicles in secret in the mid-2000s.

Such hypersonic glide vehicles are different from conventional ballistic missiles in three ways. First, they have a longer range, and can travel over more than half of the Earth circumference. Second, they can approach their target from a direction opposite to the expected trajectory of a typical ballistic missile, and do so on a low altitude gliding trajectory within the atmosphere. Third, they can be extremely precise, with terminal guidance systems enabling them to strike with an accuracy of a few meters. These characteristics make such vehicles nearly impossible to detect. Though it will take many more years and billions more dollars to complete the project, upon completion such missiles could effectively decimate a country's nuclear and military arsenals in a few tens of minutes, using low-yield nuclear weapons or even conventional explosives. During the

"Weaponization and Outer Space Security," by Nayef Al-Rodhan, *Global Policy Journal*, March 12, 2018. Reprinted by permission.

Cold War, Russia and the US avoided serious nuclear escalations because the involved weapons on both sides could inflict severe damage on the entire world. However, the precision of hypersonic weapons eradicates this deterrent. Russia has already responded by creating the Aerospace Defence Forces in 2015, tasked with protecting the country against the Prompt Global Strike.

As other countries start to consider the US's weaponization programmes threatening—the US military space budget is estimated at $25 billion and possibly even at more than $40 billion—they are taking steps to defend themselves. Hypersonic missiles rely on satellites to function properly and for this reason both Russia and China are increasingly developing the capacity to destroy US satellites. Destroying a satellite could render the US military both blind and deaf, subsequently obscuring the precise targeting capabilities of hypersonic missiles for moving targets, which require a steady stream of data.

Given these latest developments, the need for the establishment and maintenance of space as a global commons is critical to global peace and security. Here, it is necessary to distinguish between using space for military purposes (such as using satellites to guide the military or collect intelligence) and the physical placing of weapons in space to target locations or objects on Earth and in space. The problem with the latter is that there is no globally agreed upon definition of what space weapons are. Most space technology has multiple purposes, making it harder to monitor, and complicating the issue of space weaponization and defining weapons under space law.

Space Weapons

The term "space weapons" encompasses both weapons placed in space and those on Earth capable of targeting space assets, as well as weapons that transit in outer space. Such weapons include satellites that can fire lasers, or rockets capable of launching satellites from the Earth into the low-Earth Orbit (LEO). France, Russia, China, the US, Ukraine, India, and Japan have such capabilities, and North

Korea and Iran are not far behind. As satellites are instrumental to a nation's military and its economy, demolishing them can serve the military objectives of an adversary. Most space-faring countries have their own launch capabilities and more than 50 countries have their own satellites or own a large percentage of shares in a satellite. In addition, the United States, Russia, France, Germany, Italy, Japan, China, India and Israel possess their own reconnaissance satellites. Reconnaissance satellites are observation or communication satellites deployed for military or intelligence purposes.

Moreover, the United States, China, Russia, Japan, India and Israel are all investing in hit-to-kill systems to be used for anti-satellite (ASAT) or missile defence. The ASAT capacities of major space powers are already known. China was involved in the most high-profile incident of ASAT testing in 2007, when it used a missile to blow up one of its own defunct weather satellites in LEO. China has also made significant progress in developing anti-ballistic missiles (ABM) which like ASATs can also be used to target other state's intelligence, surveillance and reconnaissance satellites. Both the US and Russia have also successfully tested anti-satellite weaponry—the US taking down a low-orbit defunct satellite in 2008 and the Russians completing a flight test of the A-235 Nudol direct ascent anti-satellite missile. North Korea recently joined the race, launching its own satellite into space. Iran will also be on the way to improving its ASAT capabilities, if it follows through on the 2013 announcement that it is setting up a facility to track orbiting objects. Indeed, any progressions made into launching rockets into space are directly relevant to increasing a nation's capability of firing ballistic and intercontinental missiles.

There are currently several types of known space weapons and others are being invented all the time, often secretively. Scientists have already developed directed-energy weapons, such as laser and particle beams to blast energy at targets and make them inoperant. Lasers are a cost-effective method for addressing smaller threats, such as shooting down drones or stopping small ships. Lasers also decrease collateral damage, as they are very precise. Ongoing projects include that of the Defence Advanced Research Projects Agency, which is working on a weapon that will shoot molten metal, with the help of electromagnets—known as Magneto Hydrodynamic Explosive Munition (MAHEM). MAHEM can be attached to a missile and has greater control and destructiveness in hitting targets compared to existing weapons. Often militaries outsource the production of these weapons to private security firms such as Lockheed Martin, which between 2014 and 2015 conducted 60 "successful tests of a laser turret on a business jet," in addition to successful tests of laser weapons on the ground. Other examples of laser weapons include: airborne lasers (attached to Boeing 747-400 aircraft); Active Denial Technology (millimetre-wave electromagnetic waves that are not lethal but efficient in deterring adversaries by heating their skin without severe pain); and the US Army's Tactical High Energy Laser (THEL), which shoots enough energy at flying rocket warheads to cause them to detonate.

Legal Frameworks

The Outer Space Treaty of 1967, established nearly a half a century ago, remains the basic guidelines of international space law, and the most important among the UN's 5 major space treaties. However, the treaty does not prohibit the stationing of weapons in space or ASAT weapons. In fact, the development of space technologies has always been linked to military strength, especially at the time when the Outer Space Treaty was signed. The unwillingness of the signatory parties to develop their space capacities exclusively for "peaceful purposes," as stipulated in the treaty, has set a precedent for accepting militarised space use, which continues today.

In 2000, the UN adopted a resolution on the "Prevention of an Outer Space Arms Race, which re-emphasized the importance of using space for peaceful purposes, the importance of avoiding an arms race and "the readiness of all states to contribute to that common objective, in conformity with the provisions of the Treaty on Principles Governing the Activities of States in the Exploration and Use of Outer Space, Including the Moon and Other Celestial Bodies" (Annex III). The Anti-Ballistic Missile (ABM) Treaty, signed in 1972, reduced the number of ABM deployment areas down to one, constituting an important step in disarmament. However, in 2002 the US formally withdrew from the treaty, damaging international security and disarmament trends. The next day, the Kremlin announced that it would no longer abide by the second Strategic Arms Reduction Treaty (START II), signed in 1993, which established a limit on strategic weapons such as nuclear warheads, submarine-launched ballistic missiles and heavy intercontinental ballistic missiles.

There are several other treaties and numerous non-binding resolutions on the topic of space security. Some examples include the 1968 Agreement on the Return of Astronauts, the 1972 Convention on the International Liability for Damage Caused by Space Objects and the 1975 Convention on Registration of Objects Launched Into Outer Space. However, there are several looming issues. For example, there is no agreement between states on dealing with the ever increasing amount of space debris or how to distribute liability for generating space debris that damages another state's space assets. A document on "Space Debris Mitigation Guidelines of the Committee on the Peaceful Uses of Outer Space" was endorsed in 2007 by the General Assembly. It contains recommendations on how states should implement measures on debris mitigation. In 2014, the United Nations Office for Outer Space Affairs (UNOOSA) convened a compendium of space debris mitigation standards, and in 2011 the UN also made efforts to foster transparency and confidence-building in outer space activity. However such measures still have a long way to go prior to becoming legally binding.

The exportation of space technology is often classified information, making market competition more difficult. Trade treaties focusing on the simplification of trading in satellite or other space technologies would increase transparency and foster cooperation. A potential progression could come from a group of legal experts carrying out a three-year project with the aim of creating a Manual on International Law Applicable to Military Use of Outer Space (MILAMOS).

Yet for the time being there is a clear absence of a comprehensive international legal framework that can effectively restrict countries from weaponization. This legal void is in fact contributing to an unstable and unsecure space environment. Unfortunately, geopolitical realities represent a constraint to progress in international rules and regulations, and have consistently blocked the implementation of a Code of Conduct for Outer Space Activities, proposed by the EU in 2008. The dominance and strategic dependence of the US on space assets for military purpose has fostered an uneven and tense playing field, in which its rivals seek to catch up in terms of weaponization and the US seeks to maintain its dominance.

Going Forward: Recommendations

The first and most important step towards securing space security would be, of course, to ban the deployment and testing of weapons in space. However, states have difficulty resisting investments in new technologies that promise advanced capabilities. As a consequence, discouraging them may prove to be an unrealistic endeavour. For instance, some argue that kinetic technologies are developed for scientific purposes. However, states that can afford to develop this technology will most likely also seek to master the associated advanced military capabilities, at the very least in order to understand how to defend against it.

Nevertheless, a scenario of escalation cannot be ruled out. Such testing should thus be banned, as it is more likely to transform crises into war than to act purely as deterrence to developing weapons. The marginal utility of weapons testing does not offset the extreme risks that come with their existence. They enable the swift destruction of low-orbit satellites, which many states with developed space programs (not to mention private companies) now possess, which could easily provoke retaliation and escalation with the potential to quickly spiral out of control. At the same time, state leaders must understand the importance of not resorting to threats of attacking space objects. Society is reliant on space for day-to-day services, and the implications of any attacks would be severe. Even the threat of an attack can be destructive, as an adversary may seek to protect itself with a pre-emptive attack.

It is vital to use the technology we have to support peace, not threaten it. Technological developments in space help ensure terrestrial security. Global communications systems allow for instant communications and satellites, providing valuable geological and meteorological information. These capabilities could also facilitate disarmament treaties, as information about compliance is more easily gathered and exchanged. Finally, in order to increase situational awareness of space objects already in space, as well as their purposes, states should submit valid information to international institutions which can then organize the data and provide open-source information to all about the situation in space.

Ultimately, a simple yet compelling principle must guide space security and inter-state relations down here on Earth: space is either safe for all or for no one. Given the interconnected nature of space affairs, the heavy reliance on space assets and the critical role of outer space both for civilian and military purposes, a carefully managed, well regulated and cooperative framework is indispensible moving forward. Some limited competition and egoistic behaviour cannot be ruled out, but they must be well-balanced with a commitment to keeping outer space safe. This apparent tension between competition and collaboration can be managed in a framework of Symbiotic Realism—a theory of International Relations that emphasizes the egoistic, Realist features of global politics, where anarchy remains an undisputed fact, but simultaneously accounts for the interdependences created by globalization. Had states relied this heavily on outer space in the 19th century and in the first decades of the 20th century, we could have expected states to apply classical balance-of-power thinking in their management of space weapons. Today, however, that is not only more difficult, but almost self-harming as the nature and complexity of interdependencies on Earth require a more symbiotic approach to space affairs too.

Militarizing Outer Space Has Many Negative Consequences

Alexandra Gilliard

Alexandra Gilliard is a senior editor for the International Affairs Forum, where she also interviews international relations experts. She holds an MS in global studies and international relations from Northeastern University, with expertise in conflict resolution, arms control, human rights issues, and the MENA region.

In June 2018, President Trump directed General Joseph Dunford Jr., chairman of the Joint Chiefs of Staff, to begin laying the groundwork for the establishment of a new military branch—in space.

The stated purpose of the new branch of service would be to protect U.S. space interests by overseeing debris and commercial movement. Implicitly, however, this could mark the first overt step towards the militarization of space, in order to maintain global hegemony and achieve strategic dominance over rival powers like China and Russia. Both countries have civilian and military space programs of their own, but could this move by the Trump administration lead to an arms race in space?

Ultimately, the creation of a sixth branch of the U.S. Armed Forces would have to be approved by Congress—and even if it isn't, the Air Force would remain the service branch responsible for military strategy and operations in space as it is now. Regardless of what branch of the military is responsible, what are the ramifications for the militarization of space—by the United States and other powers?

"What Are the Consequences of Militarizing Outer Space?" by Alexandra Gilliard, June 10, 2019. Reprinted by permission. This article was originally published on Global Security Review at: https://globalsecurityreview.com/consequences-militarization-space/.

Protecting National Interests Extends to Outer Space

The efforts of any one state to place armaments in space would disrupt the global balance of power, and encourage others to follow suit, setting in motion a race for strategic dominance that could well lead to weapons testing and further escalation. When on actor assumes a dominant position, rival actors will need to act similarly in order to maintain deterrence and ensure the security of their respective national interests.

The rise of globalization and ever-increasing global interconnectivity has led to a dependence on space-based technology like the Global Positioning System (GPS) for everything from simple navigation to the coordination of military operations. Such a reliance has made the destruction of satellites a priority for military planners in the event of a conflict.

As the potential for space-based threats grows, more world leaders will move to protect against the potential destruction of their space-based assets by deploying the necessary technology to deter such an attack.

Challenges of Arms Control in Space

Though the United Nations has advocated for a complete ban on the armament of space, it lacks the support of the United States in related Proposed Prevention of an Arms Race in Space (PAROS) resolutions. Since the U.S. has such a well-developed military, civilian, and commercial presence in space, it would be senseless to attempt to incur a treaty without U.S. participation, as other states would still feel the need to protect their interests.

Beyond the question of U.S. participation in any international conventions, a strong space-based arms control policy would still be difficult to implement. In space, almost anything can be used as a weapon. With enough speed in orbit, an object no larger than a rock can destroy a satellite. Simply put, even if something is not designed to be a weapon, it can be used as one in space. If policymakers cannot effectively identify what constitutes a weapon in space, weapons cannot be regulated or prohibited, making verification and enforcement close to impossible.

Consequences of Armament and Aggression in Space

The consequences of weapons testing and aggression in space could span generations, and current technological advances only increase the urgency for policymakers to pursue a limitations treaty. As it stands, there are three major ramifications of a potential arms race in space:

The Destruction of Satellites

As both financial and technological barriers to the space services industry have decreased, the number of governmental and private investors with assets in space has inevitably increased. There is now an abundance of satellites in space owned by multiple states and corporations. These satellites are used to not only coordinate military actions, but to perform more mundane tasks, like obtaining weather reports, or managing on-ground communications, and navigation.

Should states begin weapons testing in space, debris could cloud the orbit and make positioning new satellites impossible, disrupting our current way of life. More pressing, however, is that if a country's satellites are successfully destroyed by an enemy state, military capabilities can be severely hindered or destroyed, leaving the country vulnerable to attack and unable to coordinate its military forces on the ground.

Diminished Future Use of Near Space

Whether caused by weapons testing or actual aggression, the subsequent proliferation of debris around the planet would damage our future ability to access space. Not only would debris act as shrapnel to preexisting assets in space, but it would also become much more difficult to launch satellites or rockets, hindering scientific research, space exploration, and commercial operations.

From the past fifty-odd years of activity in space alone, the debris left behind in Earth's orbital field has already become hazardous to spacecraft—a main reason why the U.S. and the Soviet Union did not continue with ASAT testing during the Cold War. If greater pollution were to occur, space itself could be become unusable, resulting in the collapse of the global economic system, air travel, and various communications.

Power Imbalances and Proliferation on the Ground

Only so many states currently have access to space—which means any militarization be by the few, while other states would be left to fend for themselves. This would establish a clear power imbalance that could breed distrust among nations, resulting in a more insecure world and a veritable powder keg primed for war. Additionally, deterrence measures taken by states with access to space would escalate, attempting to build up weapons caches not dissimilar to the nuclear weapons stockpiling activities of the Cold War.

In any arms race, it is inevitable that more advanced weaponry is created. Yet, this does not only pose a risk to assets in space. Should a terrestrial war break out, this weaponry may eventually be deployed on the ground, and space-faring states would be able to capitalize on the power imbalance by using these new developments against states that have not yet broken into the space industry or developed equally-advanced weaponry.

Into the Future

The militarization of space would inevitably increase the chances of war, and also threaten the industries that rely on space to carry out their daily operations. Without treaties and resolutions to regulate and limit armament in space, the international community risks facing extreme consequences. Furthermore, with the history of U.S. disinterest in UN efforts to regulate space, the implementation of a meaningful, multilateral agreement for arms control in space is unlikely.

Ultimately, the international community will need to regulate actions, militarization, and the possibility of eventual armament in space sooner rather than later in order to reduce the threat of major war, economic destruction, and global insecurity.

Chapter 3

Are Competition and Growth in Space Exploration Beneficial to Humanity?

Overview: Competition Is Heating Up in Space

Andrew Chatzky, Anshu Siripurapu, and Steven J. Markovich

Andrew Chatzky is a foreign service officer with the US Department of State. He previously was an economics writer and editor for the Council on Foreign Relations. Anshu Siripurapu covers economics, energy, and geopolitics as a writer and editor for the Council on Foreign Relations. Steven J. Markovich is a contributor to the Council on Foreign Relations' Renewing America blog.

The 1957 launch of Sputnik and subsequent Russian firsts in space convinced many U.S. policymakers that the country had fallen dangerously behind its Cold War rival. Consecutive U.S. administrations invested in education and scientific research to meet the Soviet challenge. These investments propelled the United States to victory in the so-called space race and planted the seeds for future innovation and economic competitiveness, experts say. Yet, since the 1990s, NASA's share of federal spending has waned. The U.S. private sector has ramped up investment in space, and in May 2020, astronauts launched from U.S. soil for the first time in nearly a decade on a rocket built by the company SpaceX.

Defining the Mission

The Soviet Union took the world by surprise in October 1957 with the launch of Sputnik, the first artificial satellite. In a matter of months, President Dwight D. Eisenhower and Congress initiated measures to build U.S. scientific and engineering prowess, including the creation of NASA, a civilian space exploration agency.

"Space Exploration and U.S. Competitiveness," by Steven J. Markovich, Andrew Chatzky, and Anshu Siripurapu, Council on Foreign Relations, September 23, 2021. Reprinted by permission.

Presidents have largely determined NASA's long-term missions. In May 1961—a few weeks after the Soviet Union put the first human, Yuri Gagarin, in space—President John F. Kennedy committed the United States to a lunar landing. He stressed the urgency and value of this mission in a landmark speech at Rice University: "We choose to go to the moon in this decade and do the other things, not because they are easy but because they are hard; because that goal will serve to organize and measure the best of our energies and skills; because that challenge is one that we're willing to accept, one we are unwilling to postpone, and one we intend to win."

After six successful lunar missions, NASA's manned program pulled back to Earth, while robotic programs such as Voyager and Viking continued to explore the solar system. NASA focused on sending astronauts into low Earth orbit (LEO) with the 1973 launch of Skylab, the first U.S. space station, and the Space Shuttle. The Space Shuttle served NASA for thirty years (1981–2011) and helped build the International Space Station (ISS), an orbiting laboratory that has been continuously occupied by humans since 2000. The agency has also completed a series of unmanned missions to Mars, most recently in February 2021, when it landed the *Perseverance* rover to search for signs that life previously existed on the planet.

Successive U.S. administrations have set different space goals. The George W. Bush administration pushed for a return to the moon and a trip to Mars, but President Barack Obama favored an asteroid mission. The Obama administration also set a goal of a manned mission to orbit Mars by the mid-2030s, which would require the commitment of subsequent presidents.

President Donald J. Trump's administration voiced frustration with delays in the development of Orion, a capsule that could one day take astronauts to Mars, and urged a manned return to the moon. At the same time, Trump directed the Department of Defense to create a branch of the military under the aegis of the Air Force that would focus entirely on threats from space, an indication of renewed interest in the field. In February 2020, a proposed organizational structure for the new space force was delivered to Congress. Soon after taking office, President Joe Biden's administration announced its support of a space force.

Funding NASA

Space exploration is expensive, but it is a relatively minor line item in the U.S. budget. NASA's spending peaked at almost 4.5 percent of the federal budget in 1966, declined to 1 percent by 1975, and has gradually fallen to about half a percent in recent years. (In comparison, defense spending has hovered around 20 percent of the budget in recent years.) Congress appropriated about $23 billion for NASA in 2021, an increase of roughly 3 percent from the previous year.

Due to the Space Shuttle's retirement in 2011, NASA did not have the means to send astronauts into space by itself for nearly a decade. U.S. astronauts have had to ride Russia's Soyuz capsule to the ISS—at a cost of up to $82 million per seat. In 2010, former Apollo astronauts Neil Armstrong and Eugene Cernan warned that U.S. leadership in space exploration could suffer. Such criticisms, as well as Trump's stated desire to land astronauts on the moon during his tenure, spurred the president to boost his budget requests for the agency.

Commercializing Space

Historically, 85 to 90 percent of NASA's budget went to private contractors—largely to design and manufacture rockets and spacecraft—while NASA maintained close oversight and operated the equipment. But now NASA often privatizes operations as well. Advocates of space commercialization believe private firms such as SpaceX and Orbital Sciences, both of which won contracts to ferry ISS cargo, can provide routine LEO access at a lower cost. They say NASA could then focus more on missions that push scientific and exploration frontiers. Some go further to suggest that NASA become more like the U.S. Defense Advanced Research Projects

Agency or the National Science Foundation by setting objectives, such as capturing an asteroid, and then giving grants to private firms. But critics of privatization argue that development grants and limited competition will yield scant savings. Astrophysicist Neil deGrasse Tyson believes that while private enterprises can handle routine space flight, they are unable to bear the large and unknown risks of advancing the space frontier.

In May 2020, SpaceX became the first private company to successfully ferry two NASA astronauts to the ISS, using its Falcon 9 rocket and attached Crew Dragon capsule. President Trump said the launch "makes clear the commercial space industry is the future." The astronauts safely returned to Earth in August, and in November, NASA certified SpaceX to begin routine missions. The first of these was carried out that same month, sending four astronauts—three American and one Japanese—to the ISS. Additionally, SpaceX has announced that it plans to send three space tourists to the ISS in late 2021.

NASA is also collaborating with the private sector for its Artemis program, which aims to put astronauts, including the first woman, on the moon by 2024. In April 2020, NASA announced that the human landers for the program would be developed by SpaceX; Blue Origin, owned by Jeff Bezos, founder and chief executive of Amazon; and the Alabama-based company Dynetics. The Biden administration has pledged its continued support for Artemis.

Some entrepreneurs see a commercial future in space beyond NASA contracts and satellite launches. U.S.-based Space Adventures offers customers the opportunity to orbit Earth and experience the views and weightlessness of space travel. Other firms have pursued asteroid mining, which supporters believe could supply a new abundance of precious metals and rare earth elements. Bezos has said he plans to "build a road to space" so that humans will one day be able to sustain colonies beyond Earth. Fellow billionaire Richard Branson founded the spaceflight firm Virgin Galactic, hoping to become the industry leader in a future space tourism sector.

Launching STEM Careers and Innovations

The space race of the 1960s and 1970s captured the American public's imagination like few other human endeavors. A 2009 study in the journal *Nature* found that the Apollo program had inspired half of scientists surveyed, and almost 90 percent believed that manned space exploration inspired younger generations to study science. Some evidence supports this. According to the National Science Foundation, the percentage of graduates holding bachelor's degrees in science and engineering fields peaked in the late 1960s, around the time of the moon landing, but then declined slowly for several decades before recent administrations began to reemphasize the importance of funding science, technology, engineering, and mathematics (STEM) education.

Space exploration can also foster innovation, pushing the limits of technology and requiring the collaboration of some of the brightest people across multiple disciplines. As Jim Bell, president of the Planetary Society, a nonprofit group dedicated to space exploration advocacy and education, told CFR, "When you're embarking on an enterprise that is the hardest thing to do, it often attracts the best people who are intrigued by very difficult problems and want to have a sense in purpose in applying their knowledge to something big."

Since 1976, technologies originally developed for space exploration have led to more than two thousand spinoffs when they were transferred to the private sector. Some are obvious, such as communications satellites, but other transfers are less well known. Many medical advances are derived from space technologies, such as refinements in artificial hearts, improved mammograms, and laser eye surgery. Space exploration drove the development of new materials and industrial techniques, including thermoelectric coolers for microchips; high-temperature lubricants; and a means for mass-producing carbon nanotubes, a material with significant engineering potential. Household products such as memory-foam mattresses, Bluetooth headphones, programmable ovens, vacuums, and ski apparel all trace their origins to NASA.

International Competition and Cooperation

Only the United States has sent people beyond low Earth orbit, but experts say U.S. preeminence in space could be challenged. China became the third nation to independently launch a human into orbit in 2003 and its capabilities have since grown. The People's Liberation Army is seen as a driver of the Chinese space program, the ambitions of which include sending people to the moon and building a space station. Meanwhile, India launched its first unmanned mission to Mars in late 2013, and its probe entered Mars's orbit in September 2014. The Indian Space Research Organisation has since reached an agreement with NASA on subsequent explorations of Mars. China and the United Arab Emirates successfully sent spacecraft to orbit Mars in February 2021, the same month that NASA landed its rover there; the Chinese mission includes its own robotic explorer.

Another international mission, the landing of a European Space Agency probe on a comet, attracted widespread interest in November 2014. Though the probe was unable to anchor properly due to a landing mishap, it was still able to send a large amount of valuable data to scientists. SpaceIL, an Israeli organization, launched a moon lander in early 2019 that ultimately crashed into the moon. Nevertheless, the attempt marked the first privately funded moon landing and made Israel the fourth country to attempt a soft moon landing. India became the fifth such country in September 2019, but it too failed when its lander appeared to crash into the moon.

Space can also inspire international cooperation. In 1963, during what would be his final speech before the United Nations, President Kennedy asked, "Why should the United States and the Soviet Union, in preparing for such expeditions, become involved in immense duplications of research, construction, and expenditure?"

Kennedy's vision eventually materialized with the 1975 Apollo-Soyuz Test Project, in which U.S. and Russian spacecraft docked for the first time. Today, the United States is the ISS's managing partner, leading fourteen nations in perhaps humanity's most expensive project. The space agencies of Europe, Russia, and

Japan were also important partners on robotic missions such as the Mars rovers *Spirit* and *Opportunity*. The ISS will likely deorbit in the 2020s, but many say deeper space missions will need to be international ventures.

In May 2020, NASA announced the framework for the Artemis Accords, a series of bilateral agreements with other space agencies that want to participate in the Artemis program. CFR's David P. Fidler praised the accords, writing that they "embrace rules and principles developed through multilateralism rather than a scofflaw version of American unilateralism."

The Space Force and Uncertainty Ahead

Space policy experts agree that NASA faces considerable challenges, including new budget pressures, aging infrastructure, the rise of competing spacefaring nations, and the lack of a strong national vision for human spaceflight. An independent assessment by the National Research Council in 2012 noted that a crewed mission to Mars "has never received sufficient funding to advance beyond the rhetoric stage."

The Trump administration's push to create a space force within the military could be a sign that an era of cooperation in space is ending. In response to Trump's order, Daryl G. Kimball of the Arms Control Association said, "At worst, it is the first step in an accelerated competition between the U.S., China and Russia in the space realm that is going to be more difficult to avert without direct talks about responsible rules of the road." CFR's Stewart M. Patrick agrees that "the stage could be set for a Cold War–style space race that overwhelms any multilateral cooperation."

At the same time, policymakers face a growing number of issues around NASA's present-day purpose and methods. These include how the agency should balance various goals, such as driving scientific discovery, enhancing national security, and developing innovations with commercial benefits; how large a role the private sector should play; and to what extent NASA can be a vehicle for international cooperation and diplomacy.

Despite these questions, many experts have advocated sustaining U.S. leadership in space. "I'm convinced that in this century the nations that lead in the world are going to be those that create new knowledge. And one of the places where you have a huge opportunity to create new knowledge will be exploration of the universe, exploration of the solar system, and the building of technology that allows you to do that," said former congressman and aerospace expert Robert Walker at a CFR meeting on space policy in 2013.

Increased Space Exploration Can Lead to a Better Understanding of Earth

Josie Garthwaite

Josie Garthwaite is an associate communications director for the School of Earth, Energy and Environmental Sciences at Stanford University.

Sometimes, you need to leave home to understand it. For Stanford planetary geologist Mathieu Lapôtre, "home" encompasses the entire Earth.

"We don't only look at other planets to know what's out there. It's also a way for us to learn things about the planet that's under our own feet," said Lapôtre, an assistant professor of geological sciences in the School of Earth, Energy, & Environmental Sciences (Stanford Earth).

Scientists since Galileo have sought to understand other planetary bodies through an earthly lens. More recently, researchers have recognized planetary exploration as a two-way street. Studies of space have helped to explain aspects of climate and the physics of nuclear winter, for example. Yet revelations have not permeated all geoscience fields equally. Efforts to explain processes closer to the ground—at Earth's surface and deep in its belly—are only beginning to benefit from knowledge gathered in space.

Now, as telescopes acquire more power, exoplanet studies grow more sophisticated and planetary missions produce new data, there's potential for much broader impacts across Earth sciences, as Lapôtre and co-authors from Arizona State University, Harvard University, Rice University, Stanford and Yale University argue in the journal *Nature Reviews Earth & Environment*.

"What Other Planets Can Teach Us About Earth: Stanford Researchers Explain," by Josie Garthwaite, Stanford News Service, Stanford University, March 4, 2020. Reprinted by permission.

"The multitude and variety of planetary bodies within and beyond our solar system," they write in a paper published March 2, "might be key to resolving fundamental mysteries about the Earth."

In the coming years, studies of these bodies may well alter the way we think about our place in the universe.

Alien Forms

Observations from Mars have already changed the way scientists think about the physics of sedimentary processes on Earth. One example got underway when NASA's Curiosity Rover crossed a dune field on the red planet in 2015.

"We saw that there were big sand dunes and small, decimeter-scale ripples like the ones we see on Earth," said Lapôtre, who worked on the mission as a PhD student at Caltech in Pasadena, Calif. "But there was also a third type of bedform, or ripple, that does not exist on Earth. We couldn't explain how or why this shape existed on Mars."

The strange patterns prompted scientists to revise their models and invent new ones, which ultimately led to the discovery of a relationship between the size of a ripple and the density of the water or other fluid that created it. "Using these models developed for the environment of Mars, we can now look at an old rock on Earth, measure ripples in it and then draw conclusions about how cold or salty the water was at the time the rock formed," Lapôtre said, "because both temperature and salt affect fluid density."

This approach is applicable across the geosciences. "Sometimes when exploring another planet, you make an observation that challenges your understanding of geological processes, and that leads you to revise your models," Lapôtre explained.

Planets as Experiments

Other planetary bodies can also help to show how frequent Earth-like bodies are in the universe and what, exactly, makes Earth so different from the average planet.

"By studying the variety of outcomes that we see on other planetary bodies and understanding the variables that shape each planet, we can learn more about how things might have happened on Earth in the past," explained co-author Sonia Tikoo-Schantz, a geophysics professor at Stanford Earth whose research centers on paleomagnetism.

Consider, she suggested, how studies of Venus and Earth have helped scientists better understand plate tectonics. "Venus and Earth are about the same size, and they probably formed under fairly similar conditions," Tikoo-Schantz said. But while Earth has tectonic plates moving around and abundant water, Venus has a mostly solid lid, no water on its surface and a very dry atmosphere.

"From time to time, Venus has some kind of catastrophic disruption and a resurfacing of much of the world," Tikoo-Schantz said, "but we don't see this continuous steady state tectonic environment that we have on Earth."

Scientists are increasingly convinced that water may explain much of the difference. "We know that subduction of tectonic plates brings water down into the Earth," Tikoo-Schantz said. "That water helps lubricate the upper mantle, and helps convection happen, which helps drive plate tectonics."

This approach—using planetary bodies as grand experiments—can be applied to answer more questions about how Earth works. "Imagine you want to see how gravity might affect certain processes," Lapôtre said. "Going to other planets can let you run an experiment where you can observe what happens with a lower or higher gravity—something that's impossible to do on Earth."

Core Paradox

Studies measuring magnetism in ancient rocks suggest that Earth's magnetic field has been active for at least 3.5 billion years. But the cooling and crystallization of the inner core that scientists believe sustains Earth's magnetic field today started less than 1.5 billion years ago. This 2-billion-year gap, known as the new core paradox, has left researchers puzzling over how Earth's dynamo could have started so early, and persisted for so long.

Answers may lie in other worlds.

"In our circle of close neighbors—the Moon, Mars, Venus—we're the only planet with a magnetic field that's been going strong since the beginning and remains active today," Lapôtre said. But Jupiter-sized exoplanets orbiting close to their star have been identified with magnetic fields, and it may soon be technically feasible to detect similar fields on smaller, rocky, Earth-like worlds. Such discoveries would help clarify whether Earth's long-lived dynamo is a statistical anomaly in the universe whose startup required some special circumstance.

Ultimately, the mystery around the origin and engine behind Earth's dynamo is a mystery about what creates and sustains the conditions for life. Earth's magnetic field is essential to its habitability, protecting it against dangerous solar winds that can strip a planet of water and atmosphere. "That's part of why Mars is such a dry desert compared to Earth," Tikoo-Schantz said. "Mars started to dehydrate when its magnetic field died."

Earth Everchanging

Much of the impetus to look far beyond Earth when trying to decode its inner workings has to do with our planet's restless nature. At many points in its 4.5 billion-year existence, Earth looked nothing like the blue-green marble it is today.

"We're trying to get to the point where we can characterize planets that are like the Earth, and hopefully, someday find life on one of them," said co-author Laura Schaefer, a planetary scientist at Stanford Earth who studies exoplanets. Chances are it will be something more like bacteria than E.T., she said.

"Just having another example of life anywhere would be amazing," Schaefer said. It would also help to illuminate what happened on Earth during the billions of years before oxygen became abundant and, through processes and feedback loops that remain opaque, complex life burst forth.

"We're missing information from different environments that existed on the surface of the Earth during that time period," Schaefer explained. Plate tectonics constantly recycles rocks from the surface, plunging them into the planet's fiery innards, while water sloshing around oceans, pelting down from rainclouds, hanging in the air, and slipping in rivers and streams tends to alter the geochemistry of rocks and minerals that remain near the surface.

Earth's very liveliness makes it a poor archive for evidence of life and its impacts. Other planetary bodies—some of them dead still and bone dry, others somehow akin to the ancient Earth—may prove better suited to the task.

That's part of why scientists were so excited to find, in 2019, that a rock sample collected by the Apollo 14 astronauts in 1971 may in fact hold minerals that rocketed off of Earth as a meteorite billions of years ago. "On the Moon, there is no plate tectonics or aqueous weathering," Lapôtre said. "So this piece of rock has been sitting there intact for the last few billion years just waiting for us to find it."

To be sure, planetary scientists do not expect to find many ancient Earth time capsules preserved in space. But continued exploration of other worlds in our solar system and beyond could eventually yield a small statistical sample of planets with life on them—not carbon copies of Earth's systems, but systems nonetheless where interactions between life and atmosphere can come into sharper focus.

"They're not going to be at the same stage of life as we have today on Earth, and so we'll be able to learn about how planets and life evolve together," Schaefer said. "That would be pretty revolutionary."

A Competitive Space Tourism Industry Could Benefit Science and Health Research

Nick Caplan, Andrew Winnard, and Kirsty Lindsay

Nick Caplan is a professor of aerospace medicine and rehabilitation at Northumbria University in Newcastle, UK. Andrew Winnard is a physiotherapist and a lecturer in space medicine systematic review. Kirsty Lindsay is an aerospace physiologist and charted physiotherapist.

The announcement of the draft Spaceflight Bill in the Queen's Speech will allow the development of spaceports in the UK. This could see members of the paying public launched into space as tourists, or taking sub-orbital flights from London to New York in just 45 minutes.

Such adventures will be made possible through futuristic spaceplanes, as are already in development by companies such as Virgin Galactic, that will enable us mere mortals to experience weightlessness. If this sounds only of interest to those who can afford the six-figure ticket price, it also has major implications for scientific discovery. Space travel-related research has probably already had a more substantial positive impact on your life than you realise, and this announcement could increase this still further.

Space agencies such as ESA and NASA currently provide access to simulated microgravity for scientific research using parabolic flights. These allow human physiology research to be carried out more easily than on the International Space Station, but the time spent in microgravity is very short. Spaceplanes may provide longer sessions, which could enable more comprehensive research to inform the design of experiments into the longer-term physiological changes from spaceflight.

"Space Tourism Could Help Boost Science and Health Research—Here's How," by Nick Caplan, Andrew Winnard, and Kirsty Lindsay, The Conversation, June 22, 2017. https://theconversation.com/space-tourism-could-help-boost-science-and-health-research-heres-how-79812.

Perhaps one day we will see research teams launching groups of participants to spend a few weeks or months aboard a space hotel in order to study medical interventions that would slow the ageing process on Earth, and to help the human species colonise the Moon or even Mars.

Research dating back to the early years of the space race has led to technologies that benefit us all. Many scientific discoveries have come since the arrival of inhabitable space stations that act as orbital laboratories. NASA's first space station Skylab helped understand the effects on the human body of spending months in space and paved the way for the International Space Station.

A huge number of research studies have been completed on the ISS since the year 2000 in the areas of human physiology, biology, biotechnology, physical science and earth and space science. These studies have led to discoveries such as enhanced protein crystal growth for drug development, efficient combustion of fuel droplets, and an understanding of the effects of long duration exposure to microgravity on the human body, revealing that spaceflight has effects similar to ageing on Earth.

Despite much human physiological research being carried out in space, it has one major limitation—there are simply not enough humans currently going to space to act as research participants, leading to difficulties in research design. In fact, only 550 or so humans have ever been into space since Russian cosmonaut Yuri Gagarin first orbited the Earth in 1961.

Human physiological experiments in space tend to have very small participant numbers (for example, the NASA twins study) or they have to take place over many years. Could the boom in commercial human spaceflight accelerate the speed of human physiological discoveries in space? We certainly think so.

Commercial spaceflight companies such as SpaceX and Orbital are already launching rockets taking supplies and research equipment to the International Space Station. SpaceX is developing its habitable Dragon capsule to take space tourists around the moon, with ambitions to use its sibling, Red Dragon, to land astronauts on Mars.

Others are developing sub-orbital spaceplanes, such as Virgin Galactic's SpaceShipTwo, which will enable passengers to experience microgravity for a number of minutes or travel 30 times faster between cities than passenger airlines. To safely send throngs of space tourists beyond the atmosphere, we need to understand the health implications of just getting these "non-professional" astronauts into space through new medical research, and developing spaceports will provide access to exciting new platforms to expand these frontiers of science.

A range of unknown health risks await space tourists, who are expected to be a far more health-diverse group than current astronauts. We will need to determine the effects of high g-forces on people with medical conditions, as well as in adolescents who might want to go on the ultimate school holiday adventure past the Karman line—traditionally taken as the boundary of space. It will be vital that risks to passenger health are reduced through remote physiological monitoring, and new monitoring technologies will need to withstand the high g-forces involved in launching into space.

The British government's commitment to become one of the most attractive places in the world for commercial spaceflight will allow space research to boldly go where only limited research has gone before.

International Cooperation, Not Competition, Is Necessary to Keep Space Open and Safe

Stewart Patrick

Stewart Patrick is a weekly columnist for World Politics Review *and a senior fellow at the Council on Foreign Relations. He is also the author of* The Sovereignty Wars: Reconciling America with the World.

Fifty years after *Apollo 11* astronauts first walked on the moon, the world is entering a new Space Age. Outer space, a domain once reserved for the great powers, is democratizing. New "space-faring" nations and private corporations are entering the final frontier, taking advantage of breakthrough technologies and lower financial barriers. The possibilities for humanity are immense. They include new opportunities for communication, for observing and understanding the Earth's natural systems, for exploring the solar system and the heavens beyond, for exploiting space-based resources, and for constructing planetary defense systems to protect the planet from catastrophic collisions with near-Earth objects—asteroids, comets—and other celestial hazards.

Realizing these objectives, however, will require a broad international commitment to maintaining outer space as a stable, open and rule-bound commons. Sovereign countries must collectively manage the dilemmas of growing interdependence and agree to keep their geopolitical rivalries in check. As the Earth's orbit becomes more congested, the world urgently needs a more robust regulatory regime to manage space traffic, mitigate space debris, regulate dual-use technologies like laser arrays, and maintain a sufficient radio frequency spectrum for satellite use. The primary challenge is to construct such a system without stifling private sector innovation. The second overriding objective is to ensure that intergovernmental collaboration on common space issues trumps zero-sum strategic competition.

Unfortunately, the country best placed to lead such a renaissance in multilateral cooperation, the United States, seems determined to pursue a unilateral course in outer space. In proposing his new "Space Force," President Donald Trump framed the U.S. objective as one of "dominance." More recently, ostensibly in response to China's Chang'e 4 lunar mission, Vice President Mike Pence declared a "renewed American presence" on the moon to be a "vital strategic goal." The stage could be set for a Cold War-style space race that overwhelms any multilateral cooperation.

The agenda in outer space is vast. But three areas in particular that cry out for improved international collaboration are the regulation of satellite mega-constellations, the utilization of outer space resources, and the challenge of planetary defense.

Mega-Constellations

A growing number of private corporations—ranging from SpaceX to Amazon, OneWeb, and China's iSpace—intend to create constellations of hundreds or even thousands of orbiting satellites, to provide global wireless internet coverage and other innovations. Their advent raises a host of regulatory questions, however. One uncertainty is how regulators can dissuade corporations from squatting on the available radio frequency spectrum, even prior to launching their services, to block competitors from beating them to this limited resource. This autumn, the International Telecommunication Union plans to toughen its rules so that companies can no longer use a single satellite to warehouse "radio frequency spectrum intended for hundreds or thousands of spacecraft."

Another concern is the risk that so many satellites pose for managing space traffic and the accumulation of debris. Mark Harris, writing recently in the *MIT Technology Review*, reports that deployment of all the currently planned mega-constellations "could generate over 67,000 'collision alerts' annually," forcing operators to choose between precautionary evasive maneuvers and assuming the small risk of collision.

Outer Space Mining

Multiple companies, as well as governments, are also exploring the potential for outer space mining, including of asteroids, comets and even the moon. Some mined materials, such as water that is believed to exist on the moon in the form of ice, could be used for life support or to provide propellant for space travel. Others could in principle be brought back to Earth. Goldman Sachs bullishly estimates that a single asteroid the diameter of a football field could contain up to $50 billion in platinum.

While the plummeting cost of spacecraft has lowered barriers to space mining, the legal hurdles remain considerable. Private companies naturally hope to have their mining claims and property rights recognized. International space law, however, is ambiguous. The main legal instrument, the 1967 Outer Space Treaty passed by the U.N. General Assembly, establishes a right to the free use of outer space but prohibits national appropriation and insists that the use of space must benefit mankind. How this applies to mining claims and proceeds from mining remains unclear. The 1979 Moon Agreement, also passed by the General Assembly, is even more restrictive. It defines celestial bodies as the "common heritage of mankind"—a formulation analogous to the treatment of deep seabed resources under the 1994 U.N. Convention on the Law of the Sea, which stipulates that these be shared by humanity. The Moon Agreement, despite being approved by the U.N. General Assembly, has been ratified by only eighteen countries—none of them a significant spacefaring power.

Responding to this ambiguity in unilateral fashion, the United States in 2015 passed the U.S. Commercial Space Launch Competitiveness Act. Title IV of that act—on "Space Resource Exploitation and Utilization"—establishes that U.S.-based companies have clear property rights to the resources that they extract from asteroids and do not need to share these benefits internationally. At least two countries, Brazil and Russia, have criticized the legislation. Moscow condemned America's "disrespect for international law" and its evident "policy of domination of outer space." It is unclear whether most countries will ultimately follow the U.S. lead or choose a different path.

Planetary Defense

Finally, multilateral cooperation is imperative in defending Earth from a low-probability but literally high-impact hazard—namely, collision with a space object like a large asteroid or comet. The planet has been repeatedly struck by space objects during its 4.5 billion years and will inevitably be clobbered again. In 1908, a meteor or comet exploded above a remote region of Siberia. This so-called Tunguska Event packed a wallop. Some 185 times more powerful than the atomic bomb that leveled Hiroshima, it flattened 80 million trees and generated a fireball 50 to 100 miles in diameter.

Recognizing the potential devastation that events of this sort could cause in populated areas, Congress in 2005 directed NASA to discover within 15 years 90 percent of all near-Earth objects (NEOs) at least 140 meters in diameter. The agency is behind schedule: It has discovered more than 8,500 such objects but estimates that two-thirds remain to be found. Last year, the Trump administration released an "NEO Action Plan," calling on U.S. government agencies to enhance their capabilities for detecting and tracking such objects, predicting potential collisions, deflecting or disrupting their trajectories, strengthening emergency preparedness and coordinating with international partners.

This final component—multilateral cooperation—demands greater attention. The explosion in 2013 of a 17-meter-diameter asteroid over Chelyabinsk, Russia, underscored the urgency. Its shockwave shattered windows and injured some 1,200 people across multiple cities. A larger asteroid or object striking an urban area could kill millions. Indeed, a collision with a large enough meteor would be an extinction-level event, like the impact that likely wiped out the dinosaurs.

In the face of a possible planetary calamity, there should be a collective response based on common humanity, rather than calculations of pure national interest. The most iconic image from those Apollo missions, after all, showed just how fragile the Earth looks from the depths of space. Its national borders are invisible, and the Earth instead is a single body. A humanity united in purpose remains an implausible prospect, of course, but it is still worth striving for at the dawn of another Space Age.

The Relationship Between the US and China in Space Demonstrates the Risks Involved in Competition

Gidon Gautel

Gidon Gautel is currently an analyst in the space industry. He was previously the project coordinator of China Foresight and project manager of the Economic Diplomacy Commission at LSE IDEAS, the London School of Economics's policy think tank.

On March 18th, 2021, NASA's Space Launch System (SLS) core stage fired its four RS-25 engines for more than 8 minutes, burning through enough Hydrolox to create its own rain clouds, and marking a key milestone on the way to bringing American astronauts back to the moon. Just months before, China's Chang'e 5 probe bounced across Earth's atmosphere at 11 km/s, safely returning 1.7 kg of lunar regolith back to Earth after a mere 22 days.

These are the dramatic scenes of the world's two superpowers pushing scientific and technological boundaries in an endeavour to explore and develop beyond the Kármán line, the 100 km atmospheric boundary that delineates the edge of space. Whilst these efforts are largely in the pursuit of scientific knowledge and—in the case of each country's commercial space industry—profit, geopolitics have always been a factor, and are increasingly holding sway. This has prompted popular commentary to brand the increasingly competitive dynamics between the US and China in this sphere as a "new space race."

Geopolitical competition and technological progress in space are closely intertwined and feed into each other. In some cases, competition drives technological change and programme decision making, most obviously in military space applications, but also

"Coordination Failure: Risks of US-China Competition in Space," by Gidon Gautel, LSE IDEAS, April 29, 2021. Reprinted by permission.

in the execution of "national pride" projects often associated with crewed spaceflight. In others, technological developments impact the intensity of terrestrial competition and inter-state tensions.

US-China competition as it relates to space, as in other areas, may take two forms. In a mode of healthy competition, the two country's race to expand humanity's celestial boundaries will drive technological and scientific innovation, with clear derivable benefits on Earth. Should such competition turn ugly, however, it may hinder scientific and technological progress in space, with detrimental consequences not just for the US and China, but for all actors with an interest in outer space, that is, almost everyone else.

This Strategic Update seeks to outline and call attention to two high-risk flash points arising from the development of the US and China's national space programmes and industries. These are the roll-out of broadband mega-constellations and increasing activities in extra-terrestrial geographically concentrated sites of interest. These risks are highlighted primarily for the consideration of third parties to great power competition, be that nations with strong interests in space, or organisations active in, or reliant on, the industry. This serves the purpose of risk mitigation and highlighting the need for international coordination.

This piece endeavours to be observational and speculative, not judgemental. It is, on the whole, a good thing that the world's two great superpowers are seeking to push humanity's boundaries in space. This, however, comes with inevitable geopolitical risks, two of which this piece seeks to identify and discuss.

The Current State of the USA's and China's Space Programmes

The United States is, and has been for the last 50 odd years, the world's largest space power. Its national programmes are overseen and executed by NASA, which wields an annual budget of north or south of $23 billion.[1] The US has recently formed the US Space Command and Space Force, which act as the country's space combatant command and service branch respectively. NASA and the US military have traditionally relied on a broad network of contractors, with companies such as Boeing, Lockheed Martin and Northrop Grumman being household names.

NASA is a scientific powerhouse, delivering a plethora of projects and engaging in countless cases of international cooperation. Its current flagship programme, however, is Artemis, an effort to create a sustainable crewed presence on the lunar surface and in orbit, enabling the development of a cis-lunar economy as well as future deep space missions, most prominently a crewed mission to Mars. The US is currently aiming for a crewed lunar landing in 2024, establishing a "Lunar Gateway"—a space station in the moon's orbit—in tandem. A surface base camp is planned for the late 2020s. These timelines, especially the 2024 landing, are likely to slip. However, a crewed landing is very likely this decade.

In recent years, NASA has increased its reliance on a broader range of commercial actors to deliver its programmes. This was done in a bid to increase competition amongst contractors, as well as NASA's number of fall-back options, in order to push down costs and prevent programme disruption. This, amongst other factors, has driven the considerable growth of the commercial space industry in the US, with innovative companies such as SpaceX pushing the envelope on what will be possible in the current decade. In 2019 alone, the US saw upwards of $4.6 billion in seed and venture investment into American space companies.[2]

China's space programme development warrants considerable praise and respect. From launching its first satellite in 1970 (12 years after the US), China now regularly tops the charts for most annual orbital launches. China is one of only three countries to return a lunar sample to Earth, one of three with an operational heavy lift launch vehicle, and the first to operate a rover on the far side of the moon. This year, it will establish its own modular orbital space station. The country's national programme is overseen and executed by the China National Space Administration (CNSA), with a budget around half that of NASA's, at upwards of $10 billion.[3] China's military space activities are spearheaded by the PLA's Strategic Support Force, a theatre command-level organisation tasked with centralising space functions, alongside cyber, electronic and psychological warfare.[4]

In 2017, China's State Council outlined the intention to establish a robotic lunar research station,[5] and this vision was expanded in 2021, when China and Russia announced an MOU indicating the intention to develop the International Lunar Research Station (ILRS).[6] More details surrounding China's future plans for its space programme are likely to be revealed some time after the launch of the first module of its orbital space station in late April 2021, likely after the station goes into full service. However, the announcement of a crewed lunar landing by the early 2030s, with the intention to establish a permanent surface and orbital presence, seems very likely.

CNSA and the PLA primarily rely on the state-owned China Aerospace Science and Industry Corporation (CASIC) and the China Aerospace Science and Technology Corporation (CASC) for the technical execution of projects. While China has its own burgeoning private space industry, strongly encouraged by the CCP, purely commercial actors do not currently play a major role in the delivery of agency programmes, certainly not to the same degree as in the United States. Investment is growing quickly, however, with $314.2 million flowing into Chinese ventures during 2019, a 10% increase to the year prior, and growth rates likely to match or exceed this in future.[7]

Mega-Constellations

As of April 2021, SpaceX has launched upwards of 1,300 Starlink satellites into low earth orbit (LEO). OneWeb, its closest competitor, has launched over 140. These satellite systems seek to provide global broadband satellite internet coverage, initially by bouncing data back and forth between users and "gateways"—terrestrial ground stations that act as conduits for data flows. Users will purchase a terminal—a receiver and supporting equipment—for connectivity. Later phases of these constellations seek to establish inter-satellite optical links, increasing bandwidth, and reducing latency and the need for ground infrastructure.

Little publicised in Western nations is the fact that at least one organisation based in China is also likely to be a major player in the provision of mega-constellation-enabled global broadband. CASC and CASIC are each developing their own constellations, named Hongyan and Hongyun respectively. Additionally, Galaxy Space, a private company founded in 2018 and backed enthusiastically by the CEO of Xiaomi is seeking to develop its own commercial constellation. Further, recent comments by officials, alongside representatives of CASC and CASIC indicate that Hongyun and Hongyan may be folded into a multi-phase mega-constellation named Guowang, which would seemingly be operated by a newly formed SOE of the same name. ITU filings regarding this latest development indicate a possible constellation of just under 13,000 satellites.[8]

The Hongyan, Hongyun and Galaxy Space constellations have all launched successful technology demonstrators, and the organisations behind them have indicated they intend to begin building out their systems in 2021. CASC's Hongyan and CASIC's Hongyun constellations were primarily envisioned to serve the PLA, rural customers within China, and overseas Chinese assets. However, announcements of the larger Guowang constellation hint at potential broader state ambitions. Furthermore, Galaxy Space's CEO, Xu Ming, has signalled the intention to rival the likes of OneWeb and SpaceX, alongside state players.[9]

Most of these constellations' early customers are likely to be national entities such as airlines, maritime users and militaries. However, all were established with the express aim of improving internet access to those with poor connections and connecting the "other three billion," the almost 50% of the Earth's population yet unconnected to the internet. Should one or more of these companies succeed in developing cheap user terminals, large new markets will be available to them. Initially, retail customers will be domestic—American and Chinese users seeking to get online or improve their connection. However, as these entities seek to expand their user base, they may increasingly compete over the same customers abroad.

This process could prove fraught. Hongyun and Hongyan (and Guowang, when/if it is formed) are state-owned. Galaxy Space's satellites are being developed in collaboration with CASC and the China Electronics Technology Corporation (CETC), both of which are SOEs.[10] This fact could well raise similar concerns from the US as those over Huawei once these constellations begin to seek global customers. One could well imagine, for example, the US objecting to allies, trade partners, or both, allowing market access to Galaxy Space, or other Chinese constellations, on the grounds of security concerns. Even where security concerns may be questionable in their foundation, what country uses which constellation could still be a geopolitical issue, with the US and China backing their own national players. Should Galaxy Space or others be able to provide a cheaper service through state backing, this would prove particularly contentious to the US and would likely raise all too familiar calls of unfair competition.

Should such tensions arise, they would be detrimental for several reasons. Firstly, this would likely place unpleasant pressure on countries not particularly aligned with the US or China, but nonetheless considered strategically important by both (most likely overwhelmingly in the Global South) to choose sides. This would degrade their sovereignty and potentially force them to make unpleasant trade-offs in the important endeavour to connect their citizens.

Secondly, the expansion of such constellations against the backdrop of geopolitical tensions increases risks around the generation of space debris. Should the rollout of mega-constellations become geopolitically confrontational, actors may become less likely to coordinate their respective systems, share information, and take precautionary measures to prevent satellite collisions. The possibility also exists for actors, in a race for market share, to cut corners in ensuring their satellites deorbit in a reasonable period of time or can be removed from orbit should they fail. This coordination failure and corner-cutting would be extremely dangerous. As has been pointed out by many concerned parties, increased and escalating in-space collisions risk the development of a catastrophic chain reaction of collisions, known as Kessler Syndrome. This, in the worst-case, would make LEO unusable, and would make it difficult, if not impossible, for humans to launch spacecraft beyond orbit without significant risk of damage.

All this considered, several lessons can be drawn. Nations considering allowing market access to a LEO broadband provider should recognise early on that they may well be making a geopolitical decision. On the other end of the transaction, one must consider the case of OneWeb, which saw the UK Government becoming one of its shareholders following the company's 2020 bankruptcy, quite possibly to prevent OneWeb's UK-based assets being acquired by a Chinese company.[11] The UK Government must recognise that a company in which it has a direct shareholder interest may one day be competing directly with a Chinese state-backed entity for foreign market share. Most crucially, however, all actors with an interest in space must put pressure on, and encourage, nations hosting constellation operators to coordinate to the greatest degree possible. This is particularly pertinent in the case of the US and China, where such coordination may be hindered by general geopolitical tensions, and more specific sensitivities in regard to the rollout of these systems. The need for greater coordination among mega-constellation (and smaller system) operators has already been widely noted, but the potential for geopolitics to make this more difficult warrants attention and highlights the particular need for the US and China, as major hosts of constellation operators, to be brought together.

[...]

Notes

1. Foust, Jeff. (2020). "NASA receives $23.271 billion in fiscal year 2021 omnibus spending bill," Space News, 21 December. Available at: https://spacenews.com/nasa-receives-23-271-billion-in-fiscal-year-2021-omnibus-spending-bill/ (Accessed 5 April 2021)

2. BryceTech. (2020). "Start Up Space 2020." Available at: https://brycetech.com/reports/report-documents/Bryce_Start_Up_Space_2020.pdf (Accessed 5 April 2021)

3. Kumar, Chethan. (2020). "Space race: China in orbit with 7 times more funding," Times of India, 1 February. Available at: https://timesofindia.indiatimes.com/business/india-business/space-race-china-in-orbit-with-7-times-more-funding/articleshow/73824661.cms (Accessed 5 April 2021)

4. Office of the Secretary of Defense. (2020). "Annual Report to Congress: Military and Security Developments Involving the People's Republic of China 2020."

5. http://www.gov.cn/xinwen/2017-11/23/content_5241782.htm (Accessed 5 April 2021)

6. http://www.gov.cn/xinwen/2021-03/09/content_5591869.htm (Accessed 5 April 2021)

7. BryceTech. (2020). "Start Up Space 2020." Available at: https://brycetech.com/reports/report-documents/Bryce_Start_Up_Space_2020.pdf (Accessed 5 April 2021)

8. Jones, Andrew. (2021). "China is developing plans for a 13,000-satellite megaconstellation," Space News, 21 April. Available at: https://spacenews.com/china-is-developing-plans-for-a-13000-satellite-communications-megaconstellation/ (Accessed 21 April 2021)

9. https://baijiahao.baidu.com/s?id=1656168054037282206&wfr=spider&for=pc (Accessed 5 April 2021)

10. Jones, Andrew. (2020). "China launches Yinhe-1 commercial low Earth orbit 5G satellite," Space News, 16 January. Available at: https://spacenews.com/china-launches-yinhe-1-commercial-low-earth-orbit-5g-satellite/ (Accessed 5 April 2021)

11. Gautel, Gidon. (2020). "Geopolitical Bickering Threatens to Spill Over into Satellite Broadband Mega-constellations," Medium, May 2020. Available at: https://medium.com/@g.gautel/geopolitical-bickering-threatens-to-spill-over-into-satellite-broadband-mega-constellations-6fbea4269e06 (Accessed 19 April 2021)

Current Controversies

Chapter 4

Are Space Tourism and Militarization Financially Feasible?

Overview: The American Public's Opinions About Space Have Shifted Over 50 Years

Courtney Johnson

Courtney Johnson formerly served as a research associate with the Pew Research Center, where she focused on science and society.

This week marks the 50th anniversary of the Apollo 11 moon landing, which was the first time humans set foot on the moon. The United States remains the only country to have put people on the moon, and, as of 2018, the large majority of Americans consider it essential that the U.S. continue to be a leader in space exploration. However, many Americans do not think future manned trips to the moon—or to Mars—should be a high priority for NASA. Instead, they put higher priority on other roles, such as monitoring Earth's climate or asteroids that could hit Earth.

Here are six Pew Research Center findings about Americans' views of space travel.

1

Most Americans think sending astronauts to Mars or the moon should be a lower priority for NASA—or say it should not be done at all. While a majority of Americans (58%) said in a 2018 survey that human astronauts are essential to the future of the U.S. space program, less than one-in-five describe sending human astronauts to Mars (18%) or the moon (13%) as top priorities for NASA. Americans are more likely to rate these goals as "important but lower priorities" (45% and 42%, respectively), or to say they are not important or should not be done at all (37% and 44%).

NASA has not put a human on the surface of the moon since the Apollo 17 mission in 1972. But just last month, NASA announced

"How Americans See the Future of Space Exploration, 50 Years After the First Moon Landing," by Courtney Johnson, Pew Research Center, July 17, 2019. Reprinted by permission.

plans to put the first woman on the moon in 2024 as part of the Artemis program. The program also aims to put human beings on the surface of Mars by the 2030s.

2

Americans see priorities other than a moon or Mars landing as more pressing for NASA. About six-in-ten (63%) say one of the organization's top priorities should be using space to monitor key parts of Earth's climate system. About four-in-ten or more said other top priorities should include conducting basic scientific research to increase knowledge of space (47%) and developing technologies that could be adapted for other uses (41%).

3

Half of Americans think space travel will become routine during the next 50 years of space exploration. Private companies like Virgin Galactic and SpaceX have plans to take tourists on suborbital space flights in the future. NASA also recently announced that it would open the International Space Station up for tourists. For now, these trips will be prohibitively expensive for the average person—for example, Virgin Galactic's tickets cost about $250,000, and NASA estimates one trip to the space station would cost about $58 million. Still, half of Americans expect space travel to become routine by 2068.

However, even if space travel does become commonplace, more than half of Americans (58%) say they would not be interested in going. People who aren't interested in orbiting the Earth in a spacecraft cite a number of concerns, including thinking it would be too expensive or scary or that their health or age would not allow for safe travel. Among the 42% who would be interested, the most common reason is that they want to experience something unique.

4

A majority of Americans say the U.S. must remain a global leader in space exploration, and that NASA's continued involvement is essential. The large majority of Americans (72%) say it is essential that the U.S. continue to be a world leader in space exploration; just 27% say it is not essential. This sentiment is shared equally across generations and among Republicans and Democrats.

A majority of Americans (65%) also describe NASA's continued involvement in space exploration as essential. Another 33% say that private companies will ensure that enough progress is made in space exploration, even without NASA's involvement. Democrats and Democratic-leaning independents (70%) are more likely than Republicans and Republican-leaning independents (59%) to say NASA must continue playing a role in space exploration. Conversely, Republicans (41%) are more likely than Democrats (28%) to say private companies will ensure that enough progress is made.

5

Americans have little confidence that private space companies will minimize space debris. Just 13% of Americans say they have a great deal of confidence that private space companies will minimize the amount of human-made space debris that they put into Earth's orbit—including fragments of rockets, satellites and other human-made objects. About half (51%) of Americans say they have not too much or no confidence at all that private companies will minimize the debris they create.

Space debris, sometimes called "space junk," is a growing concern. NASA estimates that more than 23,000 pieces of space debris 10 centimeters or larger are orbiting the Earth, and these objects could damage important spacecraft like the International Space Station.

While Americans are skeptical that private companies will limit the debris they create, they are more confident that these firms will make a profit: 44% say they have a great deal of confidence that companies like SpaceX, Blue Origin or Virgin Galactic will do this, and another 36% say they have a fair amount of confidence.

6

Americans are not enthusiastic about the idea of creating a military Space Force. The U.S. Department of Defense has long had satellites orbiting Earth, and the notion of a larger American military presence in space has been around since the 1960s. While President Donald Trump has talked about creating a Space Force as an entirely new branch of the military, most members of the public are not on-board with this plan: A May 2019 Pew Research Center survey found 36% of Americans approve of creating a military Space Force, while 60% disapprove. U.S. military veterans are more evenly split on this idea, but still more disapprove (53%) than approve (45%).

Public-Private Partnerships in Space Can Benefit Corporations and the Government

Rebecca van Burken

Rebecca van Burken is a policy analyst and senior fellow with the Reason Foundation. Her work focuses on technology and space policy efforts.

President-elect Joe Biden will predictably distance himself from many of the Trump administration's policies and positions, but its openness to commercial space partnerships should not be among them.

The expansion of public-private space partnerships that began during the Obama administration has continued during the Trump administration. These public-private partnerships have helped lead to many major space successes, including crewed-launches returning to American soil through SpaceX and the first-ever civilian passenger on a private suborbital spaceflight as part of Virgin Galactic's 2019 VSS Unity SpaceShipTwo launch.

These successes, and others, reflect positively on the U.S. space sector. However, they would not have happened without the entrepreneurial nature of commercial space. Unlike government engineers and scientists, commercial space operations are not constrained by government bureaucracy nor reliant on taxpayer funding. This allows commercial space companies to explore some seemingly far-fetched ideas, like 3D printing of small rockets, a concept being pioneered by the small start-up Relativity.

Commercial space companies must also develop and maintain a competitive edge to survive in the market. Significant competition ultimately creates less-costly services that give NASA more bang for its buck when developing new technology. Competitive market

"Biden Can Utilize Space Companies and Public Private Partnerships," by Rebecca van Burken, Reason Foundation, December 14, 2020. Reprinted by permission from Reason Foundation and Reason.org.

pressures have created inspiring innovation exemplified by SpaceX's reusable rocket technology and proposals for recycling and turning discarded orbiting tanks into space stations.

Without the federal government's continued openness to commercial space, innovation and invention in the U.S. space industry could be stifled. Commercial space continues to show up when the government needs new services. Over the last few years, we have seen amazing new technologies developed to track environmental and climate concerns. This is, in part, because NASA has entered into deals with private companies like Planet that are able to analyze data collected by satellite imagery. Planet has stakes in defense satellite imagery but has expanded its portfolio to collect data for climate scientists and researchers to use. Its constellation of 120 satellites is at work photographing every portion of the world at least once a day, which provides constant and up-to-date environmental information.

By maintaining deals like that with commercial satellite companies, NASA can avoid the costs of creating its own satellite constellation and other remote sensing technology. Additionally, NASA does not need to focus its energies on updating technologies to keep up with new software and technological capabilities.

Companies that worry about competition in the market naturally reassess their services and the burden of doing this should be put on private industry, not on the government. Biden's team should seek out the most effective private partners, hiring new talent in civil programs to use these systems. This would also free up funding for crewed space exploration.

In addition to looking to develop new partnerships for space-related efforts, a Biden administration should reassess the government's old partnerships.

Prior to the election, Reuters reported that some Biden associates believe he may try to continue funding the International Space Station (ISS) beyond its planned termination in 2025. Reuters reported:

> ...Biden, on the other hand, would likely call for a delayed moonshot and propose a funding extension for the International Space Station if he wins the White House, according to people familiar with the fledging Biden space agenda. Pushing back the moon mission could cast more doubt on the long-term fate of Boeing Co's Space Launch System (SLS) rocket, just as Elon Musk's SpaceX and Jeff Bezos' Blue Origin scramble to bring rival rockets to market as soon as next year.
>
> Extending support for the space station for a decade would also be a major boost for Boeing, whose $225 million annual ISS operations contract is set to expire in 2024 and is at the depths of a financial crisis caused by the COVID-19 pandemic and the 737 MAX grounding after fatal crashes.

This directly contradicts the Trump administration's efforts to cease funding for the archaic space station by 2025. If Biden were to continue funding this aging facility via NASA it would drain funds that could be used for more important space activities, including manned missions. Commercial companies are primed and ready to take over the space station's functions, and NASA should allow them to do so.

If Biden has taxpayers and NASA continue to fund the ISS, it would most likely continue to contract with a company that is famous for draining government money—Boeing. The partnerships with Boeing are the types of space policies the incoming Biden administration should be reviewing. It should ask Congress for a Government Accountability Office audit of Boeing's work on the Space Launch System (SLS). The contract is for the development of a rocket with heavy-lift capacities that is designed to bring humans and cargo to the moon and back. Unfortunately, it has had numerous delays and cost overruns and is still not ready for a test flight, as Bloomberg reported in August:

> Boeing Co.'s Space Launch System, the largest rocket in NASA's history, will carry a price tag of at least $9.1 billion—or 30% more than the previous estimate for a key element in the agency's plan to return to the moon.

> Additionally, the costs for new ground infrastructure at Florida's Kennedy Space Center to support the deep-space exploration program has jumped to $2.4 billion, Kathy Lueders, NASA's associate administrator for human spaceflight, said in a blog post Wednesday. That's also a 30% increase, the National Aeronautics and Space Administration said in an email Thursday.
>
> While we wait for Boeing to reuse obsolete space shuttle hardware on SLS, companies like Blue Origin and SpaceX are continually reusing entire launch boosters. Biden's administration needs a real review of whether it would be more cost and time effective to work with companies like SpaceX or Blue Origin. SLS is estimated to cost NASA $1 billion or more for each launch, after having already consumed $18.3 billion since 2010. By contrast, SpaceX has had its self-funded heavy-lift rocket Starship in development since 2012 and has been doing successful prototype tests since 2019.

Another space entity that will be a key issue for the Biden administration is the military agency, U.S. Space Force, created by President Trump. *Reason* magazine had detailed the numerous reasons a Space Force should not have been created. Now that it does exist, the Space Force should be viewed as an agency that does not need to spend taxpayers' money to create its own technology for its missions. Instead, it should use the readily available market of commercial partners ready to contract services.

Space News recently reported that the Space Force is just now learning of the private sector's capabilities:

> [Gen. John "Jay"] Raymond said in years past the only commercially viable services have been space launch and communications provided by geosynchronous satellites. But the Space Force is now becoming aware of other capabilities that are being offered commercially such as space tracking data, weather data and on-orbit satellite servicing.

Raymond, chief of operations for the Space Force, has previously committed to working closely with commercial satellite companies for space-related missions. Col. Michael "Hopper" Hopkins, commander of NASA's SpaceX Crew-1 mission, was commissioned into the Space Force and began a new line of Space Force officers expected to launch to the ISS.

To facilitate continued partnerships between the Space Force and private enterprise, the Biden administration could back an initiative currently proposed to Congress that Space Force acquisitions be "speedy and agile." Flexibility for the Space Force would include pushing acquisition power to the lowest level of management and removing bureaucracy to make its programs more efficient.

We are at a pivotal moment in the space industry's history. The federal government has the opportunity to partner with space industry innovators like Elon Musk, Jeff Bezos, and Richard Branson, and ensure there's the opportunity for new space startups to emerge and add value to the market.

The other path, a government and NASA-centric approach to space, would likely stifle technological developments and breakthroughs by private companies, cost taxpayers a lot more money, and cause the United States to fall behind other nations in a number of key areas.

Tapping Space's Commercial Potential Would Make Space Exploration More Financially Sustainable

Jeff Greason and James C. Bennett

Jeff Greason is a commercial space entrepreneur, consultant, and innovator who serves as the chief technical officer (CTO) of Electric Sky, chief executive officer (CEO) of Agile Aero, and chairman of the board of the Tau Zero Foundation. James C. Bennett is a space fellow of the Economic Policy Centre, London, and a consultant on commercial space flight and project development in space and other high technology enterprises.

America's future success in space depends on restructuring our approach for financial sustainability. While NASA has contracted with the private sector for innovation and cost savings, it continues to use the same antiquated and constraining structure that was first developed for exploring space. This carries an opportunity cost that slows the private sector's plans to harness space's many viable materials and properties, compared to the pace it could attain with a more market-friendly approach. Such activities could help solve Earth's most pressing problems and foster a space industry that sustains itself financially.

Many space-based activities have commercial potential. For example:

- tapping space-based clean energy sources
- mining asteroids for useful raw materials
- developing safe venues for scientific experiments
- upcycling/sequestering hazardous but valuable debris currently in space

"The Economics of Space: An Industry Ready to Launch," by Jeff Greason and James C. Bennett, Reason Foundation, June 5, 2019. Reprinted by permission from Reason Foundation and Reason.org.

- tapping sources of water already in space, to decouple into oxygen and hydrogen for space fuels and oxidizers, and to provide radiation shielding mass
- using the low-gravity, low-temperature and other properties of space for many activities, including manufacturing and research

These endeavors—as well as our current use of space for communication, navigation, defense, etc.—argue for a change in our approach to space from the current exploration paradigm to one of commercialization. Transportation infrastructure will create the environment for private players to develop space-based industries that use commerce to greatly increase the quality of life and decrease the cost of living. The history of developing frontiers, such as the open seas via shipping practices and the American West via railroads, demonstrates the effects of this evolution in public role.

The basic infrastructure needed should be attainable in 10 to 20 years within the same budget currently appropriated to NASA, with the following features:

- Fuel depots (essentially gas stations) in an appropriate orbit
- Fuel (from water) and water itself
- A shuttle for travel to the lunar surface
- Lunar facilities, for resupply and water and aluminum mining for construction in space
- Orbital facility complex

While this list sounds ambitious, it is technologically feasible currently and would allow the private sector to develop pragmatic use for space's assets much faster than government provision. This creates a sustainable market-based economy in space that our current approach obstructs. A commerce-based structure, much like we have with the seas and airspace, in which government provides a legal framework where the private sector can flourish, would greatly advance our use of the space environment, maximizing our potential to pursue these activities. Allowing the private sector to continue to advance private launch vehicle technology, and instead spending public funds on infrastructure, not only drives efficiency but creates a financially self-sustaining commercial industry. A great deal of low-hanging fruit is available if (and only if) we make a whole-hearted decision to turn from a merely scouting and near-offshore use of space to being a spacefaring nation.

This can all happen within the current NASA budget. In a commerce-based approach, the private sector develops the space industry and NASA and other government parties buy transport and other key services, such as on-orbit facilities, as customers of the private providers. NASA has already begun buying some space transportation in this manner, just as we currently do with other transportation systems. Extending this good start and making it more consistent is the only way, within the current NASA budget, that leads to comprehensive advancement in space.

This approach does not fault NASA, the Air Force, or the other government agencies in charge of American space launch. Almost all the approaches used by cutting-edge companies like SpaceX and Blue Origin were well known to aerospace engineers and had been thoroughly discussed in aerospace engineering forums for decades. Furthermore, the decision-makers at the top of the relevant government agencies were for the most part intelligent and experienced engineering managers. This study finds the fault lies primarily in the structure of the current system itself, especially the interplay between Congress, the contractor companies, and the agencies charged with maintaining America's space capabilities. The current structure ties space development to conflicting political requirements and fails to fund projects adequately, making for suboptimal decisions by managers, administrators, and politicians. In contrast, changing to a commerce paradigm, in which government funds infrastructure, lays the foundation for a sustainably funded space industry.

Given a functioning transportation infrastructure, as the private sector develops space industry, government's role changes to fostering that industry. What space commerce needs from government is a legal framework in which to operate that defines and defends property rights and research (especially on human health in space) that leads to more diverse space activities. Taking cues from agreements on the way various nations regard the bounty of the seas, government can ensure a sustainable and equitable free market environment. With models from other frontier exploration, government should focus on creating the legal framework to allow commerce and private endeavor to flourish.

We cannot imagine how profoundly, comprehensively and quickly technological advancement—when it is commercialized—changes our everyday lives. Every single time, and by orders of magnitude, we underestimate its power to improve ordinary people's lives once it becomes widely used through commercialization. For example, we cannot each own a jet, but today almost all of us can afford a plane ticket. This is due to the tangible effects of the synergy of technology and commerce. These effects occur so universally that any discussion of new technological frontiers should assume a blind but well-grounded expectation of manifold global rewards if only we have the foresight to encourage its proliferation. Examples from sea, land and air transportation, the Digital Age and countless other endeavors prove that technology combined with commerce triggers comprehensive advancement at a lower cost. America's future success in space depends on restructuring our approach to accommodate such a vision.

Commercialization Creates a Self-Sustaining Space Industry

Despite the best current efforts of the private sector in this direction, it's not yet an industry. Yet, launch companies have managed to create a profitable service focusing on occasional launches of very high-value payloads at very high prices. For example, the geosynchronous orbital position for telecommunications is so valuable that even our current highly inefficient way of accessing it is profitable.

SpaceX's Falcon 9 launch success at one-third the price of a traditional NASA-contracted launch demonstrates the private-sector capability to fulfill many current NASA functions at a fraction of the cost. Such achievement frees up NASA to concentrate on its core research and exploration missions in space and allows the private sector to invest in self-sustaining space-based industry. Developing the industry depends on a certain amount of infrastructure, which can pay for itself by freeing up funds currently used for NASA's SLS (Space Launch System)/Orion program.

This redistribution of current NASA funding is the key to paradigm change, although there are political problems with terminating the current SLS/Orion program in closely contested states in the 2020 presidential elections—states like Alabama and Florida. A compromise solution might be to push for increased spending on commercial service purchase, while SLS proceeds to flight status since the SLS will run out of surplus Shuttle engines by the early 2020s.

Moving our funding of space activity from solely the exploration function to a mixture of privately funded commercial industry and publicly funded research is signaled by the private sector's current capabilities, and the commercial-quality resources already identified in space that the current paradigm prevents us from harnessing. Also, changing to a commercial approach allows for efficiencies such as mass production of equipment and standardized designs that can carry cargo or humans with few modifications—which is much cheaper and more effective than what we do now. No matter how much money Congress sinks into status-quo space activities now, utility will continue to decline, making funding increasingly ineffective, and keeping the U.S. space program confined. The first step in progress is systemic change, beginning with policy change. Every single change that makes space operations more like airline operations bears fruit in lower costs, and those changes, in turn, trigger further reductions in costs.

Triggering Large-Scale Advancement in Space Without Additional Federal Funding

Private sector launch allows the market to exploit every available efficiency to develop the cheapest, most effective means of space travel. When NASA becomes a paying customer of such transportation, it fosters the development of simpler and vastly cheaper launch and vessels, which are now the most expensive, difficult and complicated part of space activity. With cheaper launch comes more launch—for the same or less cost. This allows the private sector to exploit its best uses and NASA to do the same, for more NASA emphasis on research and less on transportation.

With NASA as an anchor tenant on a privately contracted space station, funding is available for infrastructure such as orbital facilities, which expands current space activities and makes them better and cheaper to accomplish. Much like the move to railroads did for U.S. exploration and settlement of the American West, transportation infrastructure levers progress in all sectors, usable for commercial, scientific and military pursuits—without increasing NASA's space activity budget. By redirecting funds, space infrastructure would likely be available by the mid-late 2020s.

The potential exponential cost reduction and technological advancement of such a paradigm shift cannot be precisely quantified. This is especially true in a frontier like space, where we have only begun to identify caches of resources and uses of physical and material properties of space. This study (https://reason.org/wp-content/uploads/economics-of-space.pdf) gives rough order of magnitude cost and timeline estimates based on our current technological capability, knowledge of space resources and current costs, with firm estimates in the near future—through about 2025, when infrastructure would be complete enough to support a fully commercial space industry. From that point, estimates are less firm as we cannot know which technologies will dominate and which additional resources and efficiencies will proliferate. New ideas will be tested and many will fail. Some companies will fold and others rise up with new perspectives. Such a pattern and outcome is consistent with past technology leaps and acquisition of frontiers. But we know from history that transportation infrastructure catalyzes economic advancement and that industries are created and sustained through private investment and commerce.

This study (https://reason.org/wp-content/uploads/economics-of-space.pdf) examines our current radical transformation in space transport as private actors and market forces have slashed the costs of accessing space. These advancements have already greatly reduced costs for not only NASA, but also civilian (mostly satellite) and military space transport as well. These cost reductions, especially for classified military applications, cannot be quantified within the current available budget breakdowns, but are likely to follow similar cost reductions to NASA's. As with other transportation industries, increasing efficiencies continue to drive down costs, but order of magnitude efficiencies come with infrastructure that can sustain a space-faring industry, where NASA and military and civilian companies become customers on private space transport, as we have seen with shipping and rail industries and even with Antarctic exploration. We argue for shifting to an approach based on our current reality of new private launch capability at a fraction of the cost of government procurement, whereby government invests in infrastructure and allows the private sector to innovate to develop efficient transportation and financially sustainable use of space resources.

Policy Recommendations to Congress

To set NASA and the U.S. space sector on the right path, we make the following recommendations:

Legal/Security Recommendations

The U.S. government should continue active planning as begun by the current Administration for the defense and internal policing of U.S.-flagged spacecraft, space stations, and extraterrestrial facilities, including consideration of creating a Coast-Guard-like constabulary service for space. The U.S. government should also create a working group, including representatives of the space development community, to examine and make recommendations on the space treaties and international legal environment as they affect the U.S. space sector. Upon its reporting, the U.S. government should give due consideration to its recommendations regarding interpreting, modifying, and/or withdrawing from existing and pending space treaties and agreements. The U.S. should begin discussions with other market-oriented, space-using nations on a multilateral agreement within or without the framework of the Outer Space Treaty, recognizing each other's property claims on space assets.

Congress should create legislation establishing U.S. recognition of transferable resource rights, analogous to private property rights, based on first capability of reaching space resources, and transferable rights to keep-away zones around space objects, consistent with international law. It should, furthermore, create safe-harbor provisions for buying, selling, and hypothecating such rights on open markets or exchanges and in commercial and financial contracts under U.S. jurisdiction without risk of prosecution for fraud, provided that such rights are appropriately registered and verified by the U.S., consistent with international law.

Procurement Policy Recommendations

The U.S. government should declare a policy of reliance on the private sector for launch operations and in-space facilities on terms and conditions similar to those of private sector users, starting with commercial resupply and crew transportation to ISS. The baseline future scenario for an ISS should be the government's letting of anchor-tenant contracts for research space in an orbital facility or facilities.

NASA missions of any sort, including science and exploration missions, should be performed whenever possible by issuing purchase orders for results, such as data gathered from specific targets under specific conditions, rather than contracting for the development of means of obtaining such data. Evidence of market failure, judged by an agency external to NASA, should be required before permitting NASA contracting for construction or operation of spacecraft.

The U.S. government should establish a working group that includes representatives of the space development community to recommend procedures and mechanisms to ensure that NASA's spaceflight and space operations research supports private sector research and development in the same way NASA and its predecessor, the N.A.C.A., support the aviation industry.

Policy Implementation Recommendations

The U.S. government, in an agency external to NASA, should establish criteria to determine when the U.S. private sector capabilities in heavy-payload launch become sufficiently reliable that NASA should establish a timetable for exiting the development of large-payload launch vehicles and winding down existing large-payload vehicle launch operations.

The government should select NASA's future exploration missions (crewed and uncrewed) so they can take on propellant from an on-orbit facility, establish advance purchase contracts that are financially trustworthy for the purchase of that propellant and, with private industry, develop standard interfaces and interconnects for the delivery of that propellant. The industry should be allowed innovative freedom to find the best delivery mechanism. Such a pilot on-orbit refueling facility should be a 10-year objective, including a government open purchase order for delivery of water to an orbital fueling facility at a fixed price equal to the effective price of fuel launched from Earth, which should be unlimited for the first 10 years of operation.

NASA, in its periodic setting of solar system research and exploration priorities, should give preference to dual-purpose probes—i.e., those that serve both scientific research goals and also provide useful scouting data for space resource harvesting, and further possible economic uses of space and its properties.

The Establishment of the Space Force Was Premature and Too Expensive

Kaitlyn Johnson

Kaitlyn Johnson is deputy director and fellow of the Aerospace Security Project at the Center for Strategic and International Studies. Her research specializes in topics such as space security, military space systems, and commercial and civil space policy.

When President Trump first mentioned the idea of creating a "Space Force" in March of this year, few people would have expected that his seemingly offhand remark would take us to the point where we are today. The administration has called on the Department of Defense (DoD) to develop plans to stand up a new military department for national security space by 2020 while the Air Force has released its own proposal for the gradual development of the Space Force. While the administration and supporters of the Space Force proposal believe a new Service would remedy the issues in our national security space enterprise, they are overstepping in their solution.

I do not disagree with the contention that the current organizational structure of national security space is problematic. Most experts have noted that space capabilities are spread unevenly throughout DoD and the Intelligence Community, without much interoperability and communication, and space authority and coordination is fragmented. As a result, there is no true military space career path and Air Force officers with no space background are often shifted into space work. Additionally, the Air Force tends to decrease space-related funding in order to support aircraft when balancing priorities. These are serious issues that need to be resolved; however, the solution is not to jump to create a new military department. DoD needs to slow down and take a deep

"Why a Space Force Can Wait," by Kaitlyn Johnson, Center for Strategic and International Studies, October 3, 2018. Reprinted by permission.

breath, evaluate the issues that are causing our national security space enterprise to falter, and develop a strategic plan to fix them. Throwing more money and even more bureaucracy at the issue is not going to help, and holding to unrealistic timelines will not allow for thorough progress reviews of incremental steps, such as establishing a space combatant command or a dedicated space acquisition and development agency.

A significant issue with developing a Space Force by 2020 is the cost needed to establish a new military department. Statements from the administration describing the Space Force as "budget-neutral" are misleading. Deputy Secretary of Defense Patrick Shanahan even noted that standing up the new Service could cost "billions," though DoD has not completed a formal cost evaluation as of yet. It is widely understood that standing up organizations in DoD is expensive. Some things are fairly certain to cost DoD: overhead costs, development of doctrine, consolidation of facilities, movement of people and families, a service academy or war college, recruiting pipelines, and of course, new uniforms. This year, DoD plans to spend about $12.7 billion on unclassified space programs. Air Force Secretary Heather Wilson recently estimated that an additional $13 billion would be needed to establish both the new Department of the Space Force and the new U.S. Space Command (SPACECOM), and to keep both operating over the next five years.

For supporters of the Space Force, it is easy to claim a low or neutral budget with the Space Force just using existing personnel and facilities to continue current operations plus a small overhead staff. However, this also assumes that the Space Force will be able to acquire all space personnel from the other Services. If asked to join the Space Force, some service members may choose not to jump ship, per say, out of loyalty to their Service, causing the Space Force to have to recruit elsewhere. With the rushed timeframe of 2020, identifying, incentivizing, and building a relationship with key space personnel in all the departments—not just the Air Force—will take time and trust. Service members will be hard-pressed to leave their Service for a new department without sufficient trust in the leaders and mission of the Space Force. Furthermore, given that the majority of space personnel are civilians or contractors, the composition of a Space Force would be unlike any other military department. If a military department is mostly staffed by non-military personnel, is that necessarily the best fit for reorganization?

Despite DoD leaders now considering space a warfighting domain, space operations mainly provide critical support to operations in all other domains. Funding for space capabilities and operations is mixed between not only the different military departments and Services, but also intelligence agencies both within and outside of DoD. Sieving the right "pieces" out of DoD—and possibly the Intelligence Community—may add further bureaucracy to these programs. More worryingly, it may not even be possible to suss out the right programs or people due to classification levels and diversification of space capabilities. A new military department would almost inevitably result in extra bureaucracy and complications amongst the Services when conducting joint operations, which would likely account for almost all of the Space Force's operations.

Re-establishing a space-focused combatant command—the first U.S. SPACECOM was disestablished in 2002—will solve many of the issues agreed upon by space experts. First, operational space authority would be consolidated and led by a four-star general. This would provide much-needed leadership and direction across DoD. A SPACECOM would also provide the opportunity to develop highly-skilled space operators and provide a clearer career path for service members interested in a career in space operations. Similar to U.S. Special Operations Command, a SPACECOM would need to be able to manage all space operations and coordinate joint operations amongst the Services. Re-establishing SPACECOM is a good first step down the path to finding out the right construct for our national security space enterprise. Policymakers and defense officials should give SPACECOM the time and resources it needs to operate efficiently over the course of a few years in order to determine its success. Rushing to establish a Space Force by

2020 does not give ample time to test and synchronize SPACECOM with the rest of the combatant commands and the Services' space infrastructures. It may well be that another organizational construct fits the bill better than a Space Force, but without first testing—and providing ample time to test—a re-established SPACECOM, policymakers will not be able to make an informed decision on how to move forward.

The administration's plan towards a Space Force also includes establishing a Space Development Agency (SDA). Modeled after the Missile Defense Agency (MDA), the SDA would act as a research, development, and acquisition agency for national security space. Currently, the MDA has acquisition authorities to both conduct its own research and development but also to coordinate different acquisition programs across the Services. An SDA would have similar authorities to coordinate development and acquisition of space assets across the Services, providing top-level leadership on space acquisitions across the Department of Defense. SPACECOM and the SDA together may be the goldilocks combination for managing our national security space enterprise.

Some analysts have noted that even if Congress passes the necessary legislation to mandate the initial reorganization of military space, it may not go far enough to guarantee a complete solution to the problem. However, the case of reorganization of special operations forces showcases that this is not necessarily true. As Alice Hunt Friend and I recently noted, Congress has recognized the incomplete structure of special operations forces and has called for a study on the issue in this year's National Defense Authorization Act. If Congress and DoD agree to re-evaluate the status of the national security space enterprise in a few years, there will be a much more efficient and successful reorganization process.

Establishing a Department of the Space Force by 2020 is rushing into an end solution without proper consideration. Although there have been several space reorganization studies in the past two decades, a comprehensive public debate of our current space capabilities and their organization is just beginning. A complication to this discussion is, of course, that many space systems and operations are classified. If creating a Space Force is a matter of inevitability, as many believe, the process should be done thoughtfully and with intention. Other solutions presented—such as SPACECOM, a Space Development Agency, the Space Operations Force, and a Space Corps—are all viable options to remedy and make DoD space operations more efficient. Perhaps it is also time to consider that perhaps this reorganization is unique and therefore should not be limited to mimicking already-existing systems.

An incremental approach to developing a comprehensive organization for our national security space enterprise is a smarter decision. Our aim as a policy community should be to evaluate all options thoroughly, hold public discourse, and develop a solution that will best support our national security space enterprise.

Billionaires Should Focus on Fixing the Earth Instead of Unsustainable Growth in Space

Tim Jackson

Tim Jackson is a professor of sustainable development and director of the Centre for the Understanding of Sustainable Prosperity (CUSP) at the University of Surrey in the UK.

Mars ain't the kind of place to raise your kids, laments the Rocket Man in Elton John's timeless classic. In fact, it's cold as hell. But that doesn't seem to worry a new generation of space entrepreneurs intent on colonising the "final frontier" as fast as possible.

Don't get me wrong. I'm no sullen technophobe. As lockdown projects go, NASA's landing of the Perseverance rover on the surface of the red planet earlier this year was a hell of a blast. Watching it reminded me that I once led a high school debate defending the motion: this house believes that humanity should reach for the stars.

It must have been around the time that Caspar Weinberger was trying to persuade President Nixon not to cancel the Apollo space programme. My brothers and I had watched the monochrome triumph of the *Apollo 11* landing avidly in 1969. We'd witnessed the near disaster of *Apollo 13*—immortalised in a 1995 Hollywood film—when Jim Lovell (played by Tom Hanks) and two rookie astronauts narrowly escaped with their lives by using the Lunar Module as an emergency life raft. We knew it was exciting up there.

I remember later going to see *Apollo 13* (the film) with a friend who wasn't born when the mission itself took place. "What did

"Billionaire Space Race: The Ultimate Symbol of Capitalism's Flawed Obsession with Growth," by Tim Jackson, The Conversation, July 20, 2021. https://theconversation.com/billionaire-space-race-the-ultimate-symbol-of-capitalisms-flawed-obsession-with-growth-164511.

you think?" I asked as we came out of the cinema. "It was OK," said my friend. "Just not very believable."

But we kids were glued to our black-and-white TV sets the entire week of the original mission. We watched in horror as CO_2 levels rose in the Lunar Module. We endured the endless blackout as the returning astronauts plunged perilously back to Earth. We held our breath with the rest of the world as the expected four minutes stretched to five and hope began to fade. It was a full six minutes before the camera finally came into focus on the command module's parachutes—safely deployed above the Pacific Ocean. We felt the endorphin rush. We knew it was believable.

That was 1970. This is now. And here I am again on the edge of another sofa, in the lingering uncertainty of the time of COVID-19, waiting for signs of arrival from another re-entry blackout on another barren rock, devoid of breathable atmosphere, 200 million miles away. And when the Perseverance Rover finally touches down on the surface of Mars: that same exhilaration. That same endorphin rush. Quite difficult to witness the jubilation behind the masks at NASA's mission control without feeling a glimmer of vicarious joy. Hope, even.

But NASA's clever science experiment is just the tip of an expansionary iceberg. A teaser, if you will, for an ambitious dream that is being driven faster and faster by huge commercial interests. A curious twist in a debate that has been raging now for almost half a century.

Growth Wars

Ever since 1972, when a team of MIT scientists published a massively influential report on the Limits to Growth, economists have been fighting about whether it's possible for the economy to expand forever. Those who believe it can, appeal to the power of technology to "decouple" economic activity from its effects on the planet. Those (like me) who believe it can't point to the limited evidence for decoupling at anything like the pace that's needed to avoid a climate emergency or prevent a catastrophic decline in biodiversity.

The growth debate often hangs on the power you attribute to technology to save us. Usually it's the technophiles arguing for infinite growth on a finite planet—sometimes putting their hopes in speculative technologies such as direct air capture or dangerous ones like nuclear power. And usually it's the sceptics arguing for a post-growth economy. But the simple division between technophiles and technophobes has never been particularly helpful. Very few growth sceptics reject technology completely. No one at all is asking humanity to return to the cave.

My own research teams at the University of Surrey have been exploring the vital role of sustainable technology in transforming the economy for almost three decades now. But we've also shown how the dynamics of capitalism—in particular its relentless pursuit of productivity growth—continually push society towards materialistic goals, and undermine those parts of the economy such as care, craft and creativity, which are essential to our quality of life.

And now suddenly, along comes a group of self-confessed technology lovers finally admitting that the planet is too small for us. Yes, you were right, they imply: the Earth cannot sustain infinite growth. That's why we have to expand into space.

Wait. What just happened? Did somebody move the goalposts? Something is wrong. Maybe it's me. One thing I know for sure. I'm no longer the same kid I was—the one from the debating society. This house believes that humanity should grow the f*** up.

Before it spends trillions of dollars littering its techno-junk around the solar system, this house believes that humanity should pay a little more attention to what's happening right here and now. On this planet.

The Human Condition

Perhaps ironically, it was from space that we saw it first. In October 1957, the Soviets sent an unmanned orbital satellite called Sputnik into space. It was one of those odd moments in history (like the coronavirus) that dramatically reshapes our social world. Sputnik kicked off the space race, intensified the arms race and heightened the cold war. It was a huge blow to US self-esteem not to be the first nation to reach space and it was the jolt it used to kickstart the Apollo Moon shot. No one likes coming second. Least of all the most powerful people on the planet.

But Sputnik also signalled the beginning of a new relationship between humanity and its earthly home. As the political philosopher Hannah Arendt remarked in the prologue to her 1958 masterpiece, *The Human Condition*, going into space allowed us to grasp our planetary predicament for the first time in history. It was a reminder that "the Earth is the quintessence of the human condition." And nature itself, "for all we know, may be unique in providing human beings with a habitat in which they can move and breathe without effort and without artifice."

Fair point. And nothing we've learned in the intervening years has changed that prognosis. Mars may be the most habitable planet in the solar system, outside our own. But it's still a very far cry from the beauty of home—whose fragility we only truly learned to appreciate fully from the images sent back to us from space.

Nature photographer Galen Rowell once called William Anders' iconic photo Earthrise—taken from the *Apollo 8* module in lunar orbit—"the most influential environmental photograph ever taken." Earthrise brought home to us, in one astonishing image, the stark reality that this shining orb was—and still is—humanity's best chance for anything that might meaningfully be called the "good life."

Its beauty is our beauty. Its fragility is our fragility. And its peril is our peril.

An Inconvenient Truth

In the very same year that Arendt published *The Human Condition*, a Shell executive named Charles Jones presented a paper to the fossil fuel industry's trade group, the American Petroleum

Institute, warning of the impact of carbon emissions from fossil fuel combustion on the atmosphere. It was early evidence of climate change.

It was also evidence, according to lawsuits now being filed by cities and states in the US, that companies like Shell knew it was happening more than 60 years ago—three decades before James Hansen's scientific testimony to Congress in 1988 brought global warming to public attention. And they did nothing about it. Worse, argue plaintiffs like the state of Delaware, they lied over and again to cover up this "inconvenient truth."

Why such a thing could happen is now clear. Evidence of their impact was a direct threat to the profits of some of the most powerful corporations on the planet. Profit is the bedrock of capitalism. And as I argue in my new book, we have allowed capitalism to trump everything: work, life, hope—even good governance. The most enlightened governments in the world have turned a blind eye to the need for urgent action. Now we're on the verge of being too late to fix it. Achieving net zero by 2050 is no longer enough. We need much more, much faster to avoid ending up in an unliveable hothouse.

Even as I write, record-breaking temperatures, 10-20°C above the seasonal average, have forced citizens on the west coast of North America into underground shelters to avoid the searing heat. Wildfires are raging in California's Death Valley, where temperatures have reached an astonishing 54°C. On the storm-struck east coast, flood waters have inundated the New York subway system. Thousands remain homeless and hundreds are still missing, meanwhile, as historic flooding across central Europe has left almost 200 people dead.

In the face of the blindingly obvious, even recalcitrant presidents and politicians are at last beginning to acknowledge the scale of the peril in which our relentless pursuit of economic growth has placed the planet. And in principle they still have time to do something about it.

As I and many colleagues have argued, the pandemic offers us a unique opportunity to fashion a different kind of economy. The 26th Conference of the Parties to the UN Climate Change Convention (COP26) in Glasgow in November 2021 could well be the place to do that. Whether that happens or not will depend as much on vision as it does on science. And on our courage to confront the inequalities of power that led us to this point.

It will also depend on us going back to first principles and asking ourselves: how exactly should we aim to live in the only habitable world in the known universe? What is the nature of the good life available to us here? What can prosperity possibly mean for a promiscuous species on a finite planet?

The question is almost as old as the hills. But the contemporary answer to it is paralysingly narrow. Cast in the garb of late capitalism, prosperity has been captured by the ideology of "growth at all costs": an insistence that more is always better. Despite overwhelming evidence that relentless expansion is undermining nature and driving us towards a devastating climate emergency, the "fairytales of eternal growth" still reign supreme.

Zero Gravity

It's an ironic twist in the tale of the debate society kid I used to be that I've spent most of my professional life confronting those fairytales of growth. Don't ask me how that happened. By accident mostly.

I toyed with the idea of studying astrophysics. But I ended up studying Maths at Cambridge, where I confess to being baffled by the complexity of it all, until I realised that even math is just a trick. Quite literally a formula. Believe in it and you can travel to the stars and back. In your mind, at least.

And there I was wandering around in zero G, when I woke up one day (in April 1986) to find that the Number four reactor at the Chernobyl nuclear power plant in Ukraine had suffered a catastrophic meltdown. I suddenly realised that the very same skills

I'd spent my life developing were leading humanity not towards the stars but away from the paradise we already inhabit.

So yes. I changed my mind. The next day I walked into the Greenpeace office in London and asked what I could do to help. They set me working on the economics of renewable energy. I became, accidentally, an economist. (Economics needs more accidental economists.) And that's when it began to dawn on me that learning how to live well on this fragile planet is far more important than dreaming about the next one.

Mine Is Bigger Than Yours

Not so the space race billionaires. A handful of unbelievably powerful men, whose wealth has exploded massively throughout the pandemic, are now busy trying to persuade us that the future lies not here on Earth but out there among the stars.

Tesla founder and serial entrepreneur, Elon Musk is one of these new rocket men. "Those who attack space," he tweeted recently, "maybe don't realise that space represents hope for so many people." That may be true of course in a world where huge inequalities of wealth and privilege strip hope from the lives of billions of people. But, as the spouse of a NASA flight controller pointed out, it obscures the extraordinary demands of escaping from Mother Earth, in terms of energy materials, people and time.

Undeterred, the rocket men gaze starward. If resources are the problem, then space must be the answer. Amazon founder Jeff Bezos is pretty explicit about his own expansionary vision. "We can have a trillion humans in the solar system," he once declared. "Which means we'd have a thousand Mozarts and a thousand Einsteins. This would be an incredible civilisation."

Bezos and Musk have spent their lockdown contesting the top two places on the *Forbes* rich list. They've also been playing "mine is bigger than yours" in their own private space race for a couple of decades now. Bezos's personal wealth almost doubled during the course of a pandemic that destroyed the lives and livelihoods of millions. He's now stepping down to spend more time on Blue

Origin, the company he hopes will deliver vast human colonies across the solar system.

The declared aim of Musk's rival company, SpaceX, is "to make humanity multiplanetary." Just like Kim Stanley Robinson's science fiction trilogy back in the 1990s, Musk aims to establish a permanent human colony on Mars. To get there, he reasons, we need very big rockets—or, in the original terminology of SpaceX, Big F***ing Rockets (BFRs)—eventually capable of transporting scores of people and hundreds of tonnes of equipment millions of miles across the solar system.

The BFRs have now given way to a series of (more sedately named) Starships. And to prove his green credentials Musk desperately wants these starships to be reusable. So much so that SpaceX conspired to blow up four consecutive Starship prototypes in quick succession during the first four months of 2021 trying unsuccessfully to re-land them.

Move fast and break things is the Silicon Valley motto of course. But eventually you've got to bring the goods home. Starship SN15 finally achieved that on May 5—three weeks after SpaceX had landed a massive US$2.9 billion contract from NASA, nudging Blue Origin into the space race shadows.

Not wanting to be outdone, Bezos came up with what he must have hoped was the ultimate comeback. When Blue Origin's New Shepard rocket—which is also reusable—made its first manned space flight on July 20, he and his brother Mark would be two of the first few passengers on board. Wow, Jeff! Kudos man! Now you really show us your *cojones*! Nobody likes coming second. Least of all the most powerful people on the planet.

But sometimes you get no choice. Out of the blue, without so much as a by-your-leave, Virgin boss Richard Branson swooped in to steal everyone's thunder. On July 11, nine days before Bezos's big day, Branson became the first ever billionaire to launch himself into space.

And for a cool US$250,000, he promised us, you too can be one of Virgin Galactic's 600 or so breathless customers, waiting to enjoy three or four weightless minutes gazing back in rapture at the planet you've left behind. Apparently, Musk has already signed up. Bezos doesn't need to. He's made his own virgin space flight now.

Prosperity as Health

The space rhetoric of the super-rich betrays a mentality that may once have served humanity well. Some would say it's a quintessential feature of capitalism. Innovation upon innovation. A driving ambition to expand and explore. A primal urge to escape our origins and reach for the next horizon. Space travel is a natural extension of our obsession with economic growth. It's the crowning jewel of capitalism. Further and faster is its frontier creed.

I've spent much of my professional life as a critic of that creed, not just for environmental reasons but on social grounds as well. The seven years I spent as economics commissioner on the UK's Sustainable Development Commission and my subsequent research at the Centre for the Understanding of Sustainable Prosperity revealed something fundamental about our aspirations for the good life. Something that has been underlined by the experience of the pandemic.

Prosperity is as much about health as it is about wealth. Ask people what matters most in their lives and the chances are that this will come out somewhere near the top of the list. Health for themselves. Health for their friends and their families. Health too—sometimes—for the fragile planet on which we live and on whose health we ourselves depend.

There's something fascinating in this idea. Because it confronts the obsession with growth head on. As Aristotle pointed out in *Nicomachean Ethics* (a book named after his physician father), the good life is not a relentless search for more, but a continual process of finding a "virtuous" balance between too little and too much.

Population health provides an obvious example of this idea. Too little food and we're struggling with diseases of malnutrition. Too much and we're tipped into the "diseases of affluence" that now kill more people than under-nutrition does. Good health depends on us finding and nurturing this balance.

This task is always tricky of course, even at the individual level. Just think about the challenge of keeping your exercise, your diet and your appetites in line with the outcome of a healthy body weight. But as I've argued, living inside a system that has its sights continually focused on more makes the task near impossible. Obesity has tripled since 1975. Almost two-fifths of adults over 18 are overweight. Capitalism not only fails to recognise the point where balance lies. It has absolutely no idea how to stop when it gets there.

You'd think our brush with mortality through the pandemic would have brought some of this home to us. You'd think it would give us pause for thought about what really matters to us: the kind of world we want for our children; the kind of society we want to live in. And for many people it has. In a survey carried out during lockdown in the UK, 85% of respondents found something in their changed conditions they felt worth keeping and fewer than 10% wanted a complete return to normal.

When life and health are at stake, the ungodly scramble for wealth and status feels less and less attractive. Even the lure of technology pales. Family, conviviality and a sense of purpose come to the fore. These are the things that many people found they lacked most throughout the pandemic. But their importance in our lives was not a COVID accident: they are the most fundamental elements of a sustainable prosperity.

The Denial of Death

Something even more surprising has emerged during my three decades of research. Behind consumer capitalism, behind the frontier mentality, beyond the urge to expand forever lies a deep-seated and pervasive anxiety.

What does day two look like, Bezos once asked a crowd of the faithful, referring to his famous maxim about the need to innovate. "Day two is stasis, followed by irrelevance, followed by excruciatingly painful decline, followed by death," he said. "And that. Is why. It is always. Day one!" His audience loved it.

Musk plays out his own inner demons just as disarmingly. "I'm not trying to be anyone's saviour," he once told TED's head curator, Chris Anderton. "I'm just trying to think about the future—and not be sad." Again, the applause was deafening.

A well-trained therapist could have a field day with all of this. Take that miraculous day a few weeks after the Perseverance rover started sending home the most amazing selfies in the universe, when the Ingenuity helicopter made its virgin flight in the wafer thin atmosphere of Mars. It was the kind of outcome that could have intelligence agencies drooling over far less benign uses of the technology. But there was also something pretty existential going on.

The faint whispering of the Martian wind, relayed faithfully across the solar system, doesn't just confirm the possibilities for aerial flight on an alien planet. It's grist to the mill of an essential belief that human beings are endlessly creative and fiendishly clever.

Our visceral response to these momentary triumphs speaks to a branch of psychology called terror management theory drawn from the work of cultural anthropologist Ernest Becker. It was explored in particular in his astonishing 1973 book *The Denial of Death*. In it, Becker argues that modern society has lost its way, precisely because we've become terrified of confronting the inevitability of our own demise.

Terror management theory tells us that, when mortality becomes "salient," instead of addressing the underlying fear, we turn for comfort to the things which make us feel good. Capitalism itself is a massive comfort blanket, designed to help us never confront the mortality that awaits us all. So too are the dreams of the rocket men.

Beyond Lockdown

When Sputnik kickstarted the first "space race" six decades ago, a US newspaper headline called it "one step toward [our] escape from imprisonment to the Earth." Arendt read those words with astonishment. She saw there a deep-seated "rebellion against human existence." It isn't just the pandemic that locks us down, the implication is. It's the entire human condition.

The anxiety we feel is nothing new. The choice between confronting our fears and running away from them has always been a profound one. It's exactly the choice we're facing now. As vaccine roll-out brings a glimmer of light at the end of COVID-19, the temptation to rush into wild escapism is massive.

But for all its glamour, the "final frontier" is at best an amusement and at worst a fatal distraction from the urgent task of rebuilding a society ravaged by social injustice, climate change and a loss of faith in the future.

With most of us still reeling from what the World Health Organisation has called a shadow pandemic in mental health, any kind of escape plan at all looks remarkably like paradise. And emigrating to Mars is one hell of an escape plan.

Let's dream of some "final frontier" by all means. But let's focus our minds too on some quintessentially earthly priorities. Affordable healthcare. Decent homes for the poorest in society. A solid education for our kids. Reversing the decades-long precarity in the livelihoods of the frontline workers—the ones who saved our lives. Regenerating the devastating loss of the natural world. Replacing a frenetic consumerism with an economy of care and relationship and meaning.

Never have these things made so much sense to so many. Never has there been a better time to turn them into a reality. Not just for the handful of billionaires dreaming of unbridled wealth on the red planet, but for the eight billion mere mortals living out their far less brazen dreams on the blue one.

Organizations to Contact

The editors have compiled the following list of organizations concerned with the issues debated in this book. The descriptions are derived from materials provided by the organizations. All have publications or information available for interested readers. This list was compiled on the date of publication of the present volume; the information provided here may change. Be aware that many organizations take several weeks or longer to respond to inquiries, so allow as much time as possible.

Canadian Space Agency (CSA)

6767 Route de l'Aéroport
Saint-Hubert, QC J3Y 8Y9
Canada
(450) 926-4800
email: www.asc-csa.gc.ca/eng/forms/information-request.asp
website: www.asc-csa.gc.ca/eng/Default.asp

The Canadian Space Agency is the official national space agency of Canada. It was established in 1990 by the Canadian Space Agency Act. The agency has played an instrumental role in developing space technology and expertise on the subject and frequently collaborates with the European Space Agency (ESA) and National Aeronautics and Space Administration (NASA).

European Space Agency (ESA)

24 Rue du Général Bertrand CS 30798
75007 Paris
France
email: education@esa.int
website: www.esa.int

The European Space Agency (ESA) is an intergovernmental organization made up of 22 European member states. Although initially its mission focused on the unmanned exploration of space, it has since worked with the International Space Station (ISS) to include human spaceflight in its flight program.

The Federation of Galaxy Explorers (FOGE)

6404 Ivy Lane, Suite 810
Greenbelt, MD 20770
(610) 981-8511
email: info@galaxyexplorers.org
website: www.galaxyexplorers.org

FOGE is an American nonprofit youth organization that aims to educate students on space and to encourage them to pursue careers in space-related science and engineering. It hosts space-themed summer camps that allow high school students to build and launch rockets. It also hosts an annual "Battle of the Rockets" competition and published the Moon Base One educational video game, which allows participants to play as an astronaut on Moon Base One.

National Aeronautics and Space Administration (NASA)

NASA Headquarters
300 E Street SW, Suite 5R30
Washington, DC 20546
(202) 358-0001
email: nssc-contactcenter@nasa.gov
website: www.nasa.gov

NASA is an agency of the US government that handles aeronautic- and space-related research as well as the country's civilian space program. NASA has been responsible for most US space exploration efforts, and its accomplishments include creating the Skylab space station, launching the space shuttle, successfully facilitating the Apollo moon landing missions, and enabling innovations in earth science through the Earth Observing System.

Nuclear Threat Initiative (NTI)

1776 Eye Street NW
Suite 600
Washington, DC 20006
(202) 296-4810
email: contact@nti.org

NTI is a nonpartisan nonprofit organization that works to shape and secure nuclear security policies. The organization specializes in research and reports on nuclear policy and helps shape international policymaking by advocating for nuclear disarmament and peace.

Space Exploration Technologies Corp. (SpaceX)

1 Rocket Road
Hawthorne, CA 90250
(310) 363-6000
email: media@spacex.com
www.spacex.com

SpaceX is an American company that manufactures aerospace technology and facilitates space transportation. It was founded in 2002 by Elon Musk with the goal of reducing the cost of space transportation and ultimately enabling the colonization of Mars. It is the first privately owned company to launch and recover an orbital spacecraft, the first to successfully reuse an orbital rocket, and the first privately owned company to send astronauts into orbit.

The Space Policy Institute (SPI)

957 E Street NW, Suite 403
Washington, DC 20052
(202) 994-1592
email: SPI@gwu.edu
website: spi.elliott.gwu.edu

The Space Policy Institute (SPI) is a part of the George Washington University Elliott School of International Affairs. It is focused on promoting research, education, and informed debate on topics related to international and domestic space policy. It hosts symposia, conferences, and seminars on space policy, and its website provides articles, papers, and presentations on this topic.

The Union of Concerned Scientists (UCS)

Two Brattle Square
Cambridge, MA 02138
(617) 547-5552
email: forms.ucsusa.org/contact/
website: www.ucsusa.org

The Union of Concerned Scientists (UCS) is an American nonprofit organization that aims to use independent scientific research to address urgent issues faced by humanity. It was founded in 1969 by a group of scientists and students from the Massachusetts Institute of Technology (MIT) and works to combine technology and advocacy to find innovative solutions.

United Nations Office for Outer Space Affairs (UNOOSA)

United Nations Office in Vienna
Vienna International Centre
Wagramerstrasse 5
A-1220 Vienna
Austria
email: www.unoosa.org/oosa/en/contact-us/index.html
website: www.unoosa.org/oosa/index.html

UNOOSA is an office of the United Nations that works to encourage international cooperation and peace in outer space. It aims to assist the United Nations Committee on the Peaceful Uses of Outer Space (COPUOS) in helping create regulations for activities in space and aiding developing countries in using space technology. It is responsible for the implementation of international space law, as dictated by international space treaties and UN General Assembly resolutions.

United States Space Force (USSF)

United States Department of the Air Force
1690 Air Force Pentagon
Washington, DC 20330
(703) 697-3039
email: www.spaceforce.mil/Contact/
website: www.spaceforce.mil

The US Space Force is a branch of the US military that is part of the Department of the Air Force and focuses on space service. It is the first independent space force in the world. Though the Space Force was only recently established as a branch of the military, its roots reach back to 1945, when the US Army Air Forces began their space programs at the beginning of the Cold War, and to the establishment of the Air Force Space Command in 1982.

Virgin Galactic

New Mexico Spaceport Authority
166 North Roadrunner Parkway, Suite 1C
Las Cruces, NM 88011
(575) 424-2100
email: virgingalacticpress@virgingalactic.com
website: www.virgingalactic.com

Virgin Galactic is a spaceflight company that was founded by Richard Branson in 2004. The company launched its first successful suborbital flight in 2018 and aims to provide commercial suborbital flights for space tourism in 2022. In July 2021, Branson became the first owner of a private spaceflight company to travel on his own ship into outer space.

Bibliography

Books

Eric Berger. *Liftoff: Elon Musk and the Desperate Early Days That Launched SpaceX*. New York, NY: William Morrow and Company, 2021.

Erik Cohen and Sam Spector, eds. *Space Tourism: The Elusive Dream* (Tourism Social Science Series). Bingley, UK: Emerald Publishing, 2019.

Christian Davenport. *The Space Barons: Elon Musk, Jeff Bezos, and the Quest to Colonize the Cosmos*. New York, NY: PublicAffairs, 2019.

Linda Dawson. *War in Space: The Science and Technology Behind Our Next Theater of Conflict* (Springer Praxis Books). London, UK: Springer Nature, 2018.

M. M. Eboch, ed. *Commercial Space Exploration* (Introducing Issues with Opposing Viewpoints). New York, NY: Greenhaven Publishing, 2018.

Jeri Freedman. *Interstellar Manned Space Flight* (Sci-Fi or STEM?). New York, NY: Rosen Young Adult, 2018.

Alexander C. T. Geppert, Daniel Brandau, and Tilmann Siebeneichner, eds. *Militarizing Outer Space: Astroculture, Dystopia and the Cold War* (Palgrave Studies in the History of Science and Technology). London, UK: Palgrave Macmillan, 2020.

Namrata Goswami and Peter A. Garretson. *Scramble for the Skies: The Great Power Competition to Control the Resources of Outer Space*. Lanham, MD: Lexington Books, 2020.

Brian Patrick Green. *Space Ethics*. Lanham, MD: Rowman & Littlefield, 2021.

Haq Kamar, ed. *Nuclear Anxiety* (At Issue). New York, NY: Greenhaven Publishing, 2021.

Albert K. Lai. *The Cold War, the Space Race, and the Law of Outer Space: Space for Peace.* Abingdon, UK: Routledge, 2021.

Roger D. Launius. *The History of Space Exploration: Discoveries from the Ancient World to the Extraterrestrial Future.* London, UK: Thames and Hudson, 2018.

Michael Spirtas, Yool Kim, Frank Camm, Shirley M. Ross, Debra Knopman, Forrest E. Morgan, Sebastian Joon Bae, M. Scott Bond, John S. Crown, and Elaine Simmons. *A Separate Space: Creating a Military Service for Space.* Santa Monica, CA: RAND Corporation, 2020.

Annette Toivonen. *Sustainable Space Tourism: An Introduction.* Bristol, UK: Channel View Publications, 2020.

Robert Zubrin. *The Case for Space: How the Revolution in Spaceflight Opens Up a Future of Limitless Possibility.* Buffalo, NY: Prometheus Books, 2019.

Periodicals and Internet Sources

Matthew Donovan, "Opinion: It's Imperative America Preserve Its Space Power Advantage," *Defense News*, April 27, 2021. www.defensenews.com/opinion/commentary/2021/04/27/its-imperative-america-preserve-its-space-power-advantage/.

Katharine Gammon, "How the Billionaire Space Race Could Be One Giant Leap for Pollution," *Guardian*, July 19, 2021. https://www.theguardian.com/science/2021/jul/19/billionaires-space-tourism-environment-emissions.

Margaret Hartmann, "Let's Get to Know Space Force, Trump's Most Misunderstood Creation," *New York*

Magazine, November 9, 2021. www. nymag.com /intelligencer/article/space-force-guide.html.

Rebecca Heilweil, "How Bad Is Space Tourism for the Environment? And Other Space Travel Questions, Answered," Vox, July 25, 2021. www.vox.com /recode/22589197/space-travel-tourism-bezos-branson -rockets-blue-origin-virgin-galactic-spacex.

W. J. Hennigan, "America Really Does Have a Space Force. We Went Inside to See What It Does," *TIME*, July 23, 2020. www.time.com/5869987/spaceforce/.

Holman W. Jenkins, Jr., "Opinion: Why Space Tourism? Because It Operates Outside of NASA," *Wall Street Journal*, July 23, 2021. www.wsj.com/articles/space -tourism-nasa-bezos-musk-branson-11627070311.

Grace Kay, "Space Tourists Fly at Their Own Risk—Nobody Is Regulating Their Safety. Experts Say Ticket-Holders Are Accepting Their Role in an 'Experiment,'" *Business Insider*, August 1, 2021. https://www.businessinsider .com/space-tourists-fly-at-their-own-risk-nobody -regulates-safety-2021-7.

Fred Kennedy, "To Colonize Space or Not to Colonize: That Is the Question (For All of Us)," *Forbes*, December 18, 2019. https://www.forbes.com/sites /fredkennedy/2019/12/18/to-colonize-or-not-to -colonize--that-is-the-question-for-all-of -us/?sh=47cc1b142367.

Tereza Pultarova, "Prince William Isn't a Fan of Space Tourism," Space.com, October 14, 2021. www.space.com /prince-william-space-tourism-save-earth-first.

Paola Rosa-Aquino, "When Can I Buy a Ticket to Space? A Guide for Non-Billionaires," *New York Magazine,* July 2, 2021. www.nymag.com/intelligencer/article/space -tourism-bezos-explainer.html.

Ramin Skibba, "2021 Was the Year Space Tourism Opened Up. But for Whom?" *Wired*, December 29, 2021. https://www.wired.com/story/2021-was-the-year-space-tourism-opened-up-but-for-whom/.

Valerie Stimac, "3 Predictions for Space Tourism in 2022," *Forbes*, January 6, 2022. https://www.forbes.com/sites/valeriestimac/2022/01/06/3-predictions-for-space-tourism-in-2022/?sh=5b49552a471c.

Rebecca van Burken, "FAA Should Encourage Private Investment to Improve Spaceports," *Reason*, January 21, 2021. www.reason.org/commentary/private-investment-can-improve-spaceports-if-faa-doesnt-block-them/.

John Venable, "America's Commercial, Exploratory, and Defense Space Programs Have Thrived Since 2017—But Regaining Space Leadership Is a Long-Term Endeavor," Heritage Foundation, October 20, 2020. www.heritage.org/defense/report/americas-commercial-exploratory-and-defense-space-programs-have-thrived-2017.

Index

L

M

N

O

P

R

S